First Chance

ROCK ROMANCE #1

Written by

A.L. Wood

CHAPTER ONE

"It's the heart afraid of breaking that never learns to dance. It is the dream afraid of waking that never takes the chance. It is the one who won't be taken who cannot seem to give. And the soul afraid of dying that never learns to live."

Bette Midler

Natalie

"*I* think I just fell head over heels in love."

That's what my best friend Layla just squealed aloud to me.

She's staring at an album cover, drooling over the lead singer of a rock band I have never heard of. Don't get me wrong I love music, I breathe music. It's a part of my soul. I just have no interest in a mainstream rock band- sell outs really. Layla tells me the band's name is Steele's Army; their lead singer Steele is her dream man. The man she would give everything up for. A man she would follow anywhere.

She mentions that they are coming to our college in Boston. Our college, the Berklee School of Music, entered some radio contest, and we won. I do not want to go but am preparing myself to. I know Layla is going to use the friend card to get me to agree to attend this sorry excuse of a concert. What's one night of putting up with shitty soulless music for my best friend?

I've known Layla my entire life. Our parents were best friends, until tragedy struck.

I hate remembering those days. It always hurts. We celebrated every birthday and holiday together as a family. Living across the street from each other our entire lives, our parents being so close to one another, we would have dinner together every night. As a family. Rotating who would host.

Until five years ago, Layla and I were staying at my house having a movie night while our parents went to a sit down fundraiser dinner raising money for abused children. Our parents were always supporting charities. They were fortunate to have money beyond their wildest dreams. I also donate quarterly, mainly to charities for children or music programs, in memoriam of them.

I still don't know all the details, nor do I want to. I think it would fuck me up even more if I did.

Recalling that night. It was late, way past our supposed bedtime, when we heard a knock at the door. I paused the movie we were watching and answered the door. It was a police officer. He introduced himself as Officer Petty's. He asked if I was Natalie Wright. That being me of course, I said yes. He then asked if Layla was there and if we would come with him.

I should have known something was wrong when he wouldn't tell us why we were on our way to the hospital. In fact, he wouldn't tell us anything at all. When you tell someone that their parents are deceased and that her best friend's parents are in surgery, you don't want them to be alone.

When we entered the ER, he asked me if I wanted to see my parents' body, that's how we broke the crushing news. There was no way that I could handle something like that, and I really didn't wish to remember my parents that way, so I hastily declined.

Firstly, I was angered at the officer then at the doctors for not being able to save them. Then anger toward the cruelty of it all. What kind of person informs a fifteen year old that she is now alone in the world like that?

Later, I had found out that the officer did try to find out if I had any next of kin, preferring that they broke the news. I remember him asking if we would like to wait in the waiting room while Layla's parents were in surgery.

Where else would we have gone?

While we sat in that waiting room nervously awaiting news from the doctors on Layla's' parents condition, what was happening slowly sunk in. I became numb just feeling a wave of emptiness wash over me, my heart detaching itself from my emotions, no longer there. I was alone. They were my only blood family. My parents were both products of a one child family and my grandparents on both sides had passed way before I had made my way into this world.

Apparently, our parents had a few drinks and thinking Layla's father was the least drunk, he drove them home. Speeding down the road, he lost control of the car causing the vehicle to crash into a guard rail, and my parents were then thrown from the car. EMTs found my parents bodies about fifty feet away from the car. They were pronounced dead on the scene. Layla's father, Brian, was going at least seventy miles an hour and not one of them were wearing seatbelts.

Layla's father and mother recovered. They had scars from the injuries, easily hidden underneath clothing, but there was more scarring. Less visible to people that I could see in their eyes every time they looked at me for the past five years.

I think that's why they took over guardianship of me, out of obligation to my parents. I could have gone to a foster home. The money would have been put away in a trust, and when I turned eighteen, I would have been discharged from the state and handed a loaded bank account.

I know they love me in their own way, but I also think the guilt ate at them so much that they did things out of both guilt and love. My parents were rich. Layla's were as well, and because of that, my life was set. I never had to worry about anything. I could do whatever I wanted with my life. I chose to go to college many miles away from home. Away from the pity stares of everyone in my home town. With Layla.

We rented an apartment instead of residing in a dorm on campus. You never knew who you'd be rooming with, and we would rather be with each other. She's the only person who never treated me differently after my parents died. People think I should hate her. Hate her parents. How could I? They were all drinking, I'm sure it wasn't the first time they risked their lives seeing who could drive instead of calling a taxi or another friend. It could have been my parents driving.

Brian didn't mean for it to happen. It was an accident, a freak-forever life changing accident.

"Nat, NATALIE!" Layla's snapping fingers in front of my eyes and yelling at me.

She's telling me we have to go shopping for new outfits for this concert. I tell her she's buying since I don't even want to go in the first place. I must have spaced off thinking of the past. It doesn't happen often because I don't let it. I try to package it in a neat little box and shove it in the back of my mind.

I can afford it, but attending wasn't my idea, and I don't go around broadcasting the total in my bank account by spending it on frivolous materialistic items. I only spend money on necessities. Things I need to get by such as; college tuition, books, materials for class, shampoo, body wash, and food. I don't believe in luxuries because there are so many people in the Godforsaken world that aren't as well off as I am.

The first clothing store Layla sees we enter. It's not a high end shop; generally, that's what Layla usually goes for. Always eager to buy the latest in designer brand clothing items. I walk around casually glancing at clothing racks. I look behind me to see if Layla has spotted anything of interest, she's looking at some purple mini-dress, which I know will be showing all of her worldly assets. There is no way I would be dressing like that. I'll take the comfortable t-shirt and jeans any day.

As Layla is in the dressing room, I start going through the sales racks, hoping to find a shirt with some kind of coverage. At about the tenth shirt, I have looked at I finally found the one. I pull it off the hanger; it's a vintage looking Tom Petty & The Heartbreakers 1978 Long After Dark tour t-shirt. It's ratty and tattered, but it's my style all the way.

Placing the now empty hanger back onto the clothing rack I go find Layla, she's standing in front of a mirror checking herself out. I too examine her. She's beautiful, not in the cheap I spent four hours doing my hair and make-up way. But the classic natural beauty. She doesn't need makeup, and her hair is always perfect long and black, reaching the middle of her back. Her beautifully tanned skin makes her features more noticeable, eyes that are an emerald green big and round shaped like almonds with long glorious eyelashes anyone would be jealous over. A small nose and high cheekbones, her mouth pink and pouty and she's a size two with close to no curves.

She doesn't need anything artificial to make her beauty stand out.

Needless to say, we are polar opposites. I look at myself in the mirror over her shoulder; I never wear make-up on my pale face. I have never seen the need to, and I have no interest in calling attention to myself. I threw my hair up in a big scraggly bun; I have pieces of hair sprouting out all over. It's a golden brown, curly with a hint of frizz and long, it reaches the top of my ass. I have round rosebud color lips and my small nose has a slight bridge, drawing my coppery brown eyes out. Size two I am not, I have wide hips and curvy love handles.

I'm not noticeable, and I plan to keep it that way.

Layla has decided on the purple mini-dress. I glance up, thanking the stars in a whisper. I was counting on spending at least two hours in here before she had made her mind up. The mini-dress is more a piece of cloth just there to cover the actual intimate body parts, but enough for anyone to make out exactly what she is hiding.

Thinking of the shirt I chose, I happen to have a kick ass pair of jeans in my closet to go with it. I will never understand people like my best friend Layla. Why would you want to spend all night at a concert in uncomfortable clothes, a chance with the band? So not worth it to me.

She's going on and on about Steele, apparently he came from nothing, the started a band and BAM! Rock-star of the charts...I drown her out. I have no care for a band who makes their money by selling bad boy images and sex, making mediocre music that means absolutely nothing.

I believe a song should touch you. Glide over your spine inducing goosebumps, with your heart pounding to the beat. Possibly bring tears to your eyes just by feeling the words. Or make you smile and set your mood for the day ahead. That is music that I listen to that I am a true fan of.

Music that I can only dream of making. Growing up, my dad listened to all the greats. Making me fall in love with them, as well. It's something I've carried with me, and I will always hold onto. It didn't matter where we were. With my dad, he was always playing music or humming a tune to a great song aloud. He is the reason why I decided to major in music.

I want to bring back that classic feel good music, the songs that make you feel like your heart has been torn away. The songs that make you feel like no matter what you have going on in your life, everything will be all right. Music is therapy, my therapy.

As we are leaving the mall, I tell Layla I will meet up with her for dinner at her favorite Italian restaurant.

I need some time alone, so I opt to walk home. These are times I know she worries about me. She'd rather be my babysitter to know that I make it through the day, so she knows that I am OK and won't harm myself. I've never given anyone cause to believe I would, but I suffer from anxiety and panic attacks.

I stress myself out over the top about everything. I worry way too much. Mostly about things, that are out of my control, my fear reaching unimaginable heights, but I still refuse to take any prescription medicine.

So I can feel numb? I would rather live in a constant state of fear and worry about everything, than spending my entire life walking around like a zombie unfeeling.

Anxiety started ruling my life. Not long after the accident. It's a difficult thing to deal with, so I have never been able to shake. When the attacks hit, I feel suffocated and unsure of how I am going to continue to keep living my life without people knowing how much it truly affects me. How debilitating it makes me feel. I use to have nightly panic attacks, it would start with a lightheadedness feeling then nausea would creep in, in turn causing me to exert my breathing then it would escalate to hyperventilating.

All the while, my heart palpitating and my fears climbing so high that these attacks seem like they will never go away.

I learned taking walks helped when I felt the familiar feelings clawing their way in. Something about the crisp, fresh air would calm me, help me rationalize my fears. Now the nightly demons are faint memories, I have been doing pretty well keeping it at bay. Generally, the monster only reveals itself when I have an emotionally charged day.

As I wander outside, I wonder what the hell I was thinking, telling Layla I would walk. I'm at least five miles from home. Luckily, the heat is bearable, and the sun is shining. Boston is a beautiful city. Full of preserved history and more than once I have walked the Freedom Trail retaining all of the knowledge. The Boston Harbor, only blocks away from me at all times, is a wonderful place to find peace when I am fighting the long ago memories.

Two hours later, I walk into our apartment, Layla's in the living room talking to some guy.

This is normal, she randomly picks guys up that she meets. I tell her it worries me, but it's her choice to make. This is how she deals. Everyone has their own vice, something they go to. A habit or an addiction maybe, to save themselves from feeling. From facing the past. I would never fight her on it because I do things too, things that she doesn't agree with. I decide to go to my room because I don't want to ruin her night by my showing my disapproval.

Our apartment is a decent size; it consists of two bedrooms and three bathrooms. We both have our own bathroom connected to our rooms, leaving a bathroom for guests. Adjacent from the living room is the eat-in kitchen, a large archway leaving an open floor plan. There is a hallway off the living room where the guest bathroom is located off to the right before our respective bedrooms. It's all pretty compact and modern with updated appliances.

I haven't had a hand in decorating. I left it all up to Layla. She doesn't have any extremely eclectic tastes. So I have trusted in her to make it feel like home in whatever way she wants. Layla and I moved in last summer, a few weeks before school started so we could get a layout of the city and where everything was located.

The only room I have somewhat touched is mine. The walls in my room are an alabaster white and bare. I have two large bay windows at the top of my queen sized bed. I usually leave the windows open allowing the breeze from the harbor to roll in. Two nightstands adorn each side of my bed. A nicely framed picture of my parents is centered on top of the right stand. On my left is the bathroom, and to my right is my six drawer dresser positioned next to my closet. It's not a mansion sized room, but it fits my needs and its mine.

I open my door and shut it, while yanking my shirt and pants off. Layla's favorite restaurant is kind of upscale so I can't go in looking like a teenage hipster. I have a few pieces of clothing, telling of my life before. Walking over to my closet, I pull the door open and grab a few items of clothing, not even checking to see that they match. I decide I'll take a quick shower and change. I hope that Layla will be ready when I am, maybe she won't take the guy with us.

Opening my personal bathroom door, I turn the shower on choosing to let the water warm up for a few minutes; usually I face a strong shock to my system by getting in and just turning the shower on. A stream of icy cold water is a fairly easy way to wake up quickly. Not taking time lingering under the showerhead, I wash my hair and body with speed and step out of the shower, drying my body off then wrapping the towel around my hair. I walk back into my bedroom.

Having sat my clothes out on my bed, I pick the black designer dress and examine it. It ends at the knee, acceptable. I throw on a pair of flesh colored hosiery and black strappy high-heels. Unwrapping my hair, I run my fingers through it, combing out any knots I find. Then grab my handbag and walk out into the living room. Layla's there alone. Thank God, I didn't want to be a third wheel making an uncomfortable dinner. She's ready, jacket, and all.

"All ready?" Layla asks.

I nod. Making my way out of our apartment while she locks up. A few seconds later, she joins me in the elevator making our decent to the lobby of our building. I question her about the new guy, she answers evasively. That's how I know it's another unserious fling. Exiting our building, we start walking to the car garage across the street.

Many college students that opt not to live on campus choose apartments here. Being in a secure and safe building, while offering a huge well lit parking lot. When we reach her car she takes her keys out of her clutch and clicks the unlock button, I climb into the passenger seat, her in the drivers. I do not drive, maybe someday, but for now my fear is much too overwhelming. Anytime I have ever tried to sit behind the wheel I freeze, my hands unable to move. When immobile it's impossible for you to steer let alone start a car.

She whips the car out of the parking lot, making me thankful for seat belts, and we head out to dinner. Throughout the drive Layla is blabbing about the concert. How she's elated the school won and how she has always wanted to see Steele's Army live.

"Their music has always been inspirational to me." Layla says as I try to hold back from laughing.

She pays no mind to me and continues off on her story.

"You know how much I love the band Nat. As my best friend, you should just go along pretending you do, as well. Try not to be a Debbie downer tonight all right?"

"I'll try, for you Lals." I say to appease her. I'll try to pretend I am enjoying myself while we are there. Layla then goes into her plan of how she's going to sneak back stage and seduce the lead singer. This isn't something that I care to hear about.

Unable to hold my interest in her going on and on about a band like a proud groupie, I stare out the window thinking of the past, the present, the future. All the while mumbling generic responses to what she's still blabbering about.

I'm positively sure that she doesn't notice.

About thirty minutes later, we pull up to Layla's favorite restaurant Antonio's. A Valet attendant opens my door before I can. Stepping out I gawk at the upscale décor. Above me is a black awning with millions of miniature golden lights hanging about like vines, recreating the starlight in the night sky.

13

Layla joins my side; no sooner than the door is open, the smell of a mixture of garlic, basil and pasta hits my senses in strong wafts. My mouth starts watering for a taste and my stomach unintentionally rumbles aloud. I look around at the restaurant I have dined at no less than fifty times, many walls are made up of wrought iron wine racks holding some of the most expensive and diversified wines in the world. Earthy Tuscan color tones are strategically placed throughout to give the atmosphere the feel that you've flown into the heart of Italy.

The hostess takes our coats and seats us in our preferred location hidden in the back. The round white covered table is sat for two, wine glasses already overturned and ready to be filled. Our waitress comes over to our table, telling us of the daily specials. We decline, already knowing what we are going to order. We get the same thing every time we dine here.

After placing our orders, I glance over to Layla and can tell she has something on her mind, she smiles a huge grin.

Fuck.

I knew this was going to happen. She's pulling the god damn best friend card out again, twice in one day. This was uncommon, even for her. So I automatically put my defenses in place.

"Nat, so about this concert, the guy you saw earlier in our apartment, I invited him. Now I know you won't date but..."

"It's not going to happen Layla, I really would rather not go but, if you insist then I am going solo."   I say with much disinterest.

"Live a little" she begs.

"Layla, you know I love you, and I would do anything for you, you don't ask for much but I'm not doing that."

She sighs, resigning her hope as she does so.

"By the way when is this concert?"

"Don't worry Nat you have two days to prepare yourself, it's on Saturday."

Fucking Great.

CHAPTER TWO

Steele

"*F*ucking College!" I scream into my cellphone.

"Ryan, I told you about the contest." Mel says dismissively.

"I am pretty sure you fucking didn't Mel." I reply, losing patience.

"Live Nation sponsored; students put in their votes for the artist they want to perform at their college, and the college who had the highest participation level won a concert by the artist they chose." Mel explains.

"Tell me Mel, why would we want to perform at a fucking college when we have worked our asses off the past eight years to sell out Madison Square Garden?" I scream back again, not letting this shit just slide under the bridge.

"Steele calm down. Think about it, this is like giving back to your fans, young adults are your biggest fan-base, they are the people buying your records, and they put you where you are. So think of it as paying them back. You go there for a week, do a show. Then interview intern candidates and then start your tour. This is just a minor bump in the road." Mel states, pleading his case.

"Mel, I'm hanging up right now. I'm going to pretend you didn't suggest that I interview anyone. This. Is. Not. My. Job. I am going to pretend you didn't just spring this shit on me. You're lucky we have a contract or you would be fucking fired."

I want to slam my cell down. Knowing it would smash it to pieces, I don't. Instead, I put my fist through my bedroom wall. I can't believe he did this to us. For Mel to wake me up at six o'clock in the morning just to tell me that we have to leave tonight to do a show in two days and then visit the damn college for a week is complete bullshit. I do the music; I pay everyone else to do the other shit. I put my heart and soul into my music. I have worked so fucking hard to get here.

All to go back to a fucking college.

I can see gossip papers now. "Steele's Army: Sales must be down, once sold out now touring colleges!"

It will be untrue of course, but what else do papers and magazines print if not anything except a rumor. We just finished an album a couple of weeks ago, our people are predicting it will top the last album we released in sales. Already set to break the charts once again. I put more of myself into these songs than any I have made before.

Knowing there is no way I can go back to sleep now, I decide to go for a run on the public beach just outside of my condominium. Every morning when we aren't on tour, I opt to take a jog on the beach. The day we cashed our first check from our recording company; I bought a condominium in Long Beach, California. It's been the closest thing to a home that I have ever had.

Something about the scent of salt in the air and the wind blowing my hair, also forcing the sand to root in every crevice always helps keep me at peace. Most days it's where I find my songs. It's also where I go to pick through my issues.

I finish my run. Figure I'll call the boys then take a shower. It is easier calling them all at once that way I can hear the "What the fucks" and the "why didn't you tell us sooner" once and then "yeah, yeah were packing. Where and what time."

So much easier.

I call them, and it goes just as I had guessed. When I hang up, I decide I should lay back down and get some rest. With all of the times I have flown, you would think it would be simple for me to just close my eyes and fall asleep. Nope. With the ear popping, and possible turbulence it always leaves my nerves a wreck.

I'm sure the press would love to run with that as a front page article, me an alpha, bad boy rock star afraid of flying. The guys know about it, so they are always trying to distract me by fucking around with fellow passengers or the flight attendants. We have to fly quite a bit, so they are always pushing that bar higher and higher. It's surprising we haven't been kicked off a flight yet.

I wake up around four leaving just enough time to pack. For me on a tour I only need enough clothes to last me a week. We do laundry runs once a week when we stay at the hotel. Also, there's not a lot of storage on a tour bus when you're housing five men. I change my now wrinkled clothes into something clean then grab my luggage and head out the door .When I get outside, the Limousine I had called for earlier is already waiting for me. Ready to take me to LAX.

We're driving throughout Los Angeles in the middle of rush hour. This is going to be a while. I take a deep breath and set my mind in the relaxed zone, the guys can always pick up on my moods, more so when I'm pissed off. And Mel has set that tone for me for today. So I try to calm down a little.

Once we get on the airplane that's it for six months. Many bands do at least a six month tour, but because we just finished an album, we're extending our tour. Our first stint is two months, and then we will head back home for three weeks and be gone for six more months. The only benefit is that the five people I do care about, my true family in every sense, is the band, and they will be with me. So I'm not leaving anything or anyone behind.

My parents are long gone. They lived long enough to see my success. They never truly cared about me, my music or my band anyway.

I snap out of the trance that I put myself in, when I see that we are approaching the airport. My door opens, and I'm at the entrance to LAX , I'm sure the guys are already at our boarding gate for Boston seeing as how they all live together and in Los Angeles they were much closer.

I grab my bag, tip the driver and walk through security, readying myself to getting fondled by a guy. Just what I need to keep this already shitty day going. I understand why they do it, fuck I wouldn't want anyone on my plane with any sort of weapon, but I'm just not comfortable with strangers touching my body. My hands are one thing; it's how I do business. I shake hands at the closing of deals, when meeting fans, but not one of them.

I pass through security like a breeze, check my luggage in and head to the boarding gate. When I get there, I see the guys sitting down waiting for our flight to be called for boarding. I walk over to join them, taking a seat and start to bullshit.

"I'm thinking we should make a bet right now on whose going to get the most pussy while we're in Boston, winner decides the losers' humiliation." Zepp declares.

"We all know Steele is going to win, and you remember the last time what he made all of us do. Do you really want to have to tell every woman you come into contact with for a week that you carry an incurable sexually transmitted disease? Because I sure the fuck don't."

I start laughing, remembering that kickass wager. No one gets a chance to answer because our flights called, we all stand up and board the plane. Seven hours later, we arrive at Logan International airport. The guys talked throughout the entire flight; they came to the conclusion that a night of partying was in order to celebrate the pre-tour, so they plan on going out after we arrive at the hotel.

We pick our luggage up at baggage claim and exit the airport. I spot our driver, band name "Steele's Army" is written on a piece of loose-leaf paper upside down, this makes me compulsively annoyed while Liam and Gage are laughing hysterically.

Zepp stands guard, ready to apologize for what is very close to coming out of my mouth; I expect perfection from everyone especially if they are working for me. We walk over to the driver; he is intimidated instantly and bows his head, lucky for him and his show of submissive behavior has me holding my lips closed tightly together. Obviously, this guy is a pushover and hadn't realized his mistake. I can be a forgiving person, when I want to.

Most people act this way when they meet us, and I can't blame him by the image we project. It suits myself and the rest of the band just fine. Making ourselves seem just out of reach to the everyday common fan, or groupie. Hell, even the press is a protective shield. Too many people in our line of business are only out to make a name for themselves or to take advantage of us.

So I am always on the defensive mode and watching, waiting for those rats to try and sneak in. Pat, our driver, introduces himself. After a few awkward moments of silence, he then opens the car door we all climb in. Leaving the airport he is taking us directly to our hotel the Ritz-Carlton, after working as hard as we have we deserve nothing but luxury and any hotel we stay at must provide nothing but. On our drive, I tell the guys I'm going to pass on their bar hopping and catch up on some much needed rest.

Also advising them they should do the same since our impromptu concert is tomorrow afternoon. Whether or not it's at some small college or an arena, we are putting on a God damn good show. After a short ride, our car arrives at the hotel. Pat opens the door for us. Grabbing my wallet, I quickly snatch out some random bills and tip our driver. We walk through the revolving doors to the front lobby of the hotel we are staying in for the next few days.

The lady at the concierge desk is flirting with me non-stop. Bluntly making it clear that she wants to fuck. Being the gentleman that I am I politely decline. Once the keys are in my hand I dish them out, and we all decide to meet up at eight in the morning, which is pretty fucking early since they will most likely be out drinking all night. I suggest that if they really have to go out, they should try to get in at a decent time.

We planned to meet in my room to have breakfast and to discuss our plans while we are here. I still haven't told them about the prospective intern we have to interview for. Choosing to call Mel after I get some substance in my stomach and some sleep, I will find out tomorrow about his qualifications for this intern and what in the fuck they are supposed to be doing with the band while on tour.

Leaving them to find their own rooms, I tell them that our bet is on and that I am doing them a favor by giving them a head start.

CHAPTER THREE

Natalie

"*You say you want me! That you need me! Then get on your fucking knees ...*"

I dislike this song to my core; I also don't want to get up out of feathery stuffed bed and shut my alarm clock off, thus shutting the horrible song off. I'm sure Layla has planned some all-out get beautified morning for this concert. But first I need to get up and shut that god-awful song off. Then coffee. My morning routine, I cannot break; Coffee, cigarette then shower and then hopefully I am awake enough to converse with Layla.

I've tried it once before, disrupting my routine. It did not end well, for Layla, or myself because she ended up talking me into meeting a blind date she had planned and failed to remind me until the very night of said blind date. I considered going, but my anxiety clammed me up. I would have embarrassed myself if I went. To say I've learned my lesson is an understatement, she called me hurt and offended when the blind date called her because I never showed.

Since then, she tries to trick me into agreeing to do things she knows I would never agree to. Nothing like a blind date, but for instance this concert, she will remind me right up to the date, and the day of she won't leave me alone. Reassurance that I will go along with whatever plan she had made for me. It's clever I'll give her that, but it's also sneaky.

Begrudgingly, I throw my comforter off my body. I put my pink fleece robe on and slide my feet into my house slippers that are located right next to my bedroom door. Walking into the kitchen to make some delicious French vanilla flavored coffee, I see that Layla isn't awake yet. A few more minutes of reprieve before I have to listen to her all day go on about the "mouth-watering" Steele.

Once that's brewing I go open the sliding glass door to our balcony, located off the living room, being that it's June the heat is already sweltering, thankfully the wind is also whirling about, making the heat bearable. I light my morning cigarette, pulling that first drag into my lungs hits the spot. The spot that has long needed to be filled. My craving has finally found its fix. I know people are always preaching, especially Layla how it "will kill me", and "do you know what poisons they put in those cancer sticks?" I do not live under a rock, and I consider myself quite intelligent. So yes, I do know what is in "those cancer sticks."

I also know that one day; it could kill me. But so could many other things.

Although today is another glorious morning where I do not care. When I breathe it in it brings a sense of calming over me. Starting in my lungs, moving outward and expanding. Somehow allowing me to feel like I breathe that much easier.

Finishing my cigarette, I butt it out then go inside to start making my coffee. This is when Layla decides to grace myself with her presence.

"You smell like smoke Nat. When are you going to stop?"

"Don't worry, I will shower before we leave today, and I'll make sure to carry hand sanitizer and breath mints. Happy?" she holds a smile tightly, I know this doesn't make her happy but because I compromise she will close those pouty lips tightly and rein in whatever lesson she wants to teach me today about cigarette production.

"Layla, I am going to shower and get dressed. We can talk about our plans for the day after. If I know you then I know you have something up your sleeve." I tell her with fake enthusiasm.

"You're going to looooovveee what I have planned Nat." She squeals with excitement.

"I'm sure I will." I mumble on my way to my bedroom.

I grab my new Tom Petty shirt that is still in the bag on my bedroom floor from yesterday. Opening my dresser drawer, I grab my favorite pair of black lace bra and panties, then my favorite pair of grungy blue jeans. There are small man-made rips in random places and the seams are fraying, but I will never get rid of these things.

In addition, they will go perfectly with my new shirt. Matching bra and panties are a small, quirky obsession of mine, they also must be comfortable. I don't want a wire digging into my ribcage or an overabundance of padding causing my chest to look like I have a pair of cone shaped boobs.   Just because I hide my body shape under excessively baggy clothes, does not mean I don't like to admire myself occasionally. To have that secret confidence underneath my clothing, increase's my self-esteem a fraction.

The bra and panties I decide on are a classic black demi cup, and matching black boy shorts that always seems to come up over my plump behind. I hang my robe on the back of my door, take my slippers off, and go to the bathroom, clothes in hand. I strip my tank, shorts off, and start the ending of my compulsive routine.

I turn the shower off and step out onto the bathroom rug. Water dripping off my body soaking the floor. I take one of the towels and twist it around my hair then take the other towel and start drying my body off. First my face then my arms one by one. My breasts then my legs until I am completely dry.

Anxious about Layla's plans, I throw my clothes on and meet her in the kitchen.

"Natty..."

She only says this when she is up to something.

"Don't be mad but I made us appointments at the salon, you know how I like to be pampered and relaxed before a concert. I thought we could make a morning of it."

And her all too familiar "You're not wearing that are you?"

"Yes." I say hesitantly questioning her judging observation," I am wearing something I feel comfortable in. You know I don't want attention so why would I dress like that's my end goal?" I always dress this way, what the hell has overcome her lately.

"Okay, Okay, I just thought when you picked up that ratty thing it was for your at home relaxed days. Nat, you have a banging body, if you would just let me..."

I cut her off right there; I can see where she plans on heading with this. Nope. Not going to happen. "Layla, I am not some socially awkward experiment. Fuck, I shouldn't even have to remind you of this. You're lucky I am even going today."

"Because you're my girl I'm going to let that slide. I know damn well you aren't an experiment. I'm your best friend, so naturally I would want the best for you. I'm just tired of you hiding yourself behind your clothes, and your unapproachable attitude. I just want the best for you Nat! I truly I do. You sell yourself so short." Layla says pleadingly.

"I don't want to go around showcasing my goods because I'm not looking for attention. You of all people know any attention is unwanted. I try every day; I just can't wear clothes like that." I say with a slight quiver in my voice.

She likes to do this a lot. Call me out and try to make me face my demons. Hiding my body is one of the many things she tries to change. I am content with the way that I am. I have goals, and I want to accomplish them without any interruption from anyone, Layla is the only one I would make a half attempt at listening to when it came to making any changes in any part of my life.

"All right, I'm going to let this argument go for the time being, but don't think that, for one second, I am done fighting with you over this. Please just consider the things I say. You know I only want the best for you and it kills me sometimes just seeing how out of touch with the rest of the world you are. You would rather sit in a room with your music then associate with anyone besides me. We are in college, live a little Nat. Go crazy, go to a party, get drunk, and fuck a stranger. I don't care but just do something that's somewhat out of control. Don't you get tired of holding those ropes so tight?" She practically cries trying to get this through to me.

I can tell I pushed her much too far. She's always staying on the outside of my boundaries that I have set. Sometimes it's just too much for her to handle. Trying to wash the slate of our current conversation, I act quickly.

"I'll think about it. Let's drop it for now, let's make our way to the salon if you ever want to get to that damned concert of yours."

"Wait until you see where I made us an appointment, "Layla says happily. She is pleased with herself about this, so I am instantly assuming she has put out quite a decent amount of money at this salon. Layla spoils herself excessively, and if I allowed her to she would do the same for me, unneeded as I feel it to be.

We make our way out of the apartment and into her Prius. She's always going on and on about how great the car is for the environment. Layla is all for world peace and going green, when given an empty ear she could load it on end about the green movement. On the drive, I turn the radio on and play with the radio stations until I hear the beat of a familiar Lumineer's song.

Now this, this is music. What music should be. In its most raw and purest form. Singing about obsessed love. How the guy will never get over this girl, not caring how badly she treats him. You can hear it in the singers' shaky voice. The emotions he has felt. A perfect example, of true musical talent. You should sing about what you know, about what you've been through. To fans that is what makes you sound so sincere that you have experienced exactly what we have, or what we could be feeling at that precise moment. As the sound is blaring from the speakers I hum along and soon Layla does, as well.

We arrive at the G2O spa and salon; I should have known Layla would book us at the most expensive and luxurious spa in all of Massachusetts. Joy, her nametag, reads, greets us and automatically knows what our plans are, it seems Layla stops here quite a bit. We're booked in the experience room, which is above the top in over-indulgence. Joy escorts us to a private changing room, there we strip out of our clothes and enclose ourselves in ivory lavish silk robes.

This room is ours alone for the next two hours; we relax on spa beds while breathing in an ice fog, which is apparently good for your respiratory system. I only know this because Layla won't shut up about it. I thought when you went to a spa it was for peace and tranquility. Not with Layla and her incessant blabbing.

We then proceed to partake in a tropical shower, separate of course. The water is room temperature cascading over my body like a rain shower and the scent is enveloping my senses, of island fruit and ocean salt water. A breeze swirls around in the air coming from a fan in the ceiling of the shower stall that can easily fit five persons my size.

Regretfully, when the shower is over I walk back to our personal changing room. Layla is already in there and fully dressed, sitting on a bench along the wall waiting for me. Just finishing putting my clothes back on a knock sounds at the door, it is Joy coming back to escort us to the salon.

As we're walking the through the hall connecting to the salon, I tell Layla "Just so you know, just because I enjoyed that immensely doesn't mean I will not plan to live without that spoiling splendor." She grins.

"Nor am I doing a drastic hair change. A light trim and wax and we are done. Got it?"

"I got yah babe. Don't be so damn uptight. I enjoyed it; you enjoyed it. There isn't anything wrong with pampering yourself occasionally. You could use it with how wound up you keep yourself."

Bitch. Always having the last word.

Approaching the salon entrance, Layla's stylist whisks her away. A woman about my age, with gorgeous cascading shiny red hair greets me. She tells me her name is Michelle and asks what I would like to have done. I repeat what I had just told Layla. Nothing drastic. A light trim and a long overdue brow wax.

My long hair has been a helpful yet convenient safety crutch. I've long hid the emotions I couldn't hide on my face behind my hair. Michelle begs me to allow her to apply some makeup. She's curious to see what she can unveil underneath. I stubbornly agree only if she stays with an all-natural look. No caked on concealer or eye shadow and absolutely no lipstick.

I am already finished when Layla comes out, my jaw drops as I see what she's done. In all of our lives, she has never once colored her hair, until today. She is wearing it very nicely. She added some bleach blonde highlights to her chocolate brown hair, cutting it a little below her shoulders. About at a loss for words. Somehow, I manage to push out a compliment. "You look amazing!"

Not able to ignore the thought in my head I bluntly ask, "Lal, this has nothing to do with that band member you were drooling over, right?"

"What? No! "She denies.

I roll my eyes at her obvious lie.

"I just thought with all the talk about change, it was time for me to take a step too."

"Liar." I say dismissing her half attempt of an excuse. Glancing at my watch, I noticed we have about a half an hour to make it to the show, even though I don't want to partake in attendance. Layla would be pissed. Probably for weeks. It is boring as hell living with a silent pissed off roommate.

"All right let's get you and your mini dress wearing ass out of here. We have somewhere to be correct?"

The auditorium is located inside of our college. We walk through the student filled halls. It seems as this is the place to be tonight. Everyone is awaiting this show that I am dreading to even be at. Making our way to the gigantic brown doors entering the auditorium, we make a pit stop just outside. The college has sat up food and drink vendors, oh and lookie there, a merchandise table.

Looking over to the table, I notice they are only selling Steele's Army labeled items. Of course, mainstream record companies and artists are always looking for ways to make a dime. I know it's normal for a concert or festival, whatever you want to call it, to sell the performing bands shirts, sweatshirts, CD's, and posters. But usually it's almost always overpriced poorly made crap. What college student can afford to spend eighty dollars on a sweatshirt carrying the band's name?

"Want anything to drink?" Layla asks, interrupting my silent bitch fest. Causing me to jump out in surprise. I hate when she sneaks up on me like that. Luckily, no one was in close enough proximity to get hit when I jumped.

"Sure grab me a sprite please." I say reaching in my purse to grab a couple of dollars to hand her, with my hand halfway out of my purse Layla stops me, placing her hand on my shoulder.

"I got this Nat, you are here for me after all." Dropping her hand, she smiles and walks over to the drink vendor.

When Layla comes back she's handing out my drink, a red solo cup, and ice filled to the brim and a couple sips worth of sprite, they surely don't spare any expense. "Benjamin should be here any second; he said he would meet us here at the entrance."

Well I guess this is the same guy who was in our apartment yesterday, the same guy I chose not to introduce myself to because I assumed that, like normal, I wouldn't be seeing him again. I don't like befriending Layla's men because I know that he's not going to be around long, and if Layla's gets her way tonight with that lead singer this is the end of the road for him. Uncomfortable situations are not my forte.

Before I could reprimand Layla, Benjamin chooses to show his face, he kisses Layla on the check, she's smiling; she seems genuinely happy. "Hey, I'm Ben," he says in an excited tone while reaching his hand out to shake mine.

"Uh Hi, I'm Natalie." I say regretfully, introducing myself. I wasn't expecting him to be so chock full of upbeat energy.

"Why don't we go in?" Layla suggests, saving me from having an awkward conversation with her temporary Beau.

I'm not a conversationalist. Meeting new people has always been difficult for me. You make friends by talking about your likes and dislikes, by spending time with each other. These are all things that are extremely hard for me to share with anyone. Friendship is not for me, Layla being my only exception.

"Yeah, that sounds like a good idea. The sooner the show starts, the sooner it's over. The sooner it's over, the faster I can leave." An anxiety laced voice pushes out of me.

We walk through the entrance; I can see they had already set the stage for the main event. The lights are on so I can see the old worn red carpet and the high vaulted ceilings that make up our auditorium. Part of the contest was that our school would be allowed to showcase its talents. Auditions were held earlier in the week; Layla had informed me. One of the bands that were chosen are on stage now. They sound pretty damn good too. Much better than I would have thought. Bet tonight, for them, will be the time or their life. Being able to open for such a chart topping band. They'll learn, after many mistakes reaching the top, isn't what it's all cracked up to be.

The school removed a couple hundred seats, of course in the front of the stage.

"At any great concert there will always be an area for the pit," Layla once said.

Her idea of a good time at the show is front and center; my idea of a great time is in the way back, taking it all in, experiencing the music, the sound rushing around me. Enclosing my soul. Closing my eyes, and just listening. Feeling the words being sung in every song.

Unfortunately, at this concert all I wish I had was ear plugs to block out the wretched music. Their songs will not touch me, nor will they compel me to feel any kind of emotion. Their songs are about the cheapening of love, selling sex and downright full of bullshit. They could have written a song about being taken advantage of, in love and trust; instead, they write a song about taking advantage of love and trust.

Every song ever written has some metaphorical meaning behind it. Songwriters have the power to move someone physically and emotionally. I just hope that every lyricist chose to use that power to showcase raw, pure and honest meanings.

I notice Layla eyeing the stage greedily, she wants up there as close as she can get to the stage. The pit is not a place for me. I would most likely embarrass myself. Probably resulting in a massive panic attack.

"Layla, I know you want to go up there, so just go with Benjamin. I will be fine." I say with an encouraging smile.

31

"You sure babe?" she asks.

"Absolutely, go. Have fun. I'll be right back there." I say pointing to the farthest row in the back.

"Find me when the shows over, or sooner if you feel like leaving earlier." I say, offering her assurance that I am fine with her leaving me alone.

"Alright. And Nat, please just try to enjoy the show. I know you're picky when it comes to music, and you will try to fight it, but just let it go. Let yourself open up and enjoy."

I make a false promise; she won't go if she had any inkling that I didn't mean it. I make my way to the back row, other students coming the opposite direction pushing their way through me to reach the pit. After many gropes and shoves I finally make it, drink in hand and still full. Sitting down I lift my legs up and prop my feet against the chair in front of me.

CHAPTER FOUR

Steele

*T*he guys and I meet for breakfast. We have about an hour to eat before we have to go back to our respective rooms, change for the show and head off to the college. There are steps that we have to take when preparing for a show, be it at a bar or in an arena. Sound check is an important part of throwing a concert. Sure, our roadies could tune every instrument for each song, making sure that every instrument is at the right volume and the microphone is loud enough so the fans can hear my voice over the music. Not trusting anyone but ourselves, the band and I would rather do it.

There are certain things we would rather be responsible for. If you want shit done right, then you must do it yourself.

I'm backstage watching some teenage band perform. Apparently, unknown to us until earlier this morning, part of the contest was to allow some of the local campus bands to open for us. There's quite a bit of talent here. None really are in our typical style though. Usually when you have another artist open for you they are at least in the same genre as you. It helps get the crowd energized, roaring with excitement to see the headliner. Unfortunately, I don't think these bands are going to cut it.

Generally, I like to be with the band doing some kind of a warm-up backstage before we go on. Nevertheless, tonight for some reason I find myself here, on the side of the stage hidden behind a thin red curtain peeking out into the crowd. For a college campus this is a pretty decent sized area, I'm betting they could entertain over a thousand people in this room alone.

I see a large throng of people near the stage, all in a massive collective group. Everyone shoving each other just to get as close as they can to the stage. People breathing down each other's necks grinding on strangers bodies. Just to be in reach of the band. It's a thrill. A rush of adrenaline when you know you've made it that far.

That close to the people who make the music. I remember being that kid once. It seems so long ago. I used to hop rusty metal fences to see my favorite bands perform at music festivals, or if there was no way that I was getting in, I would sit outside the venue, on a sidewalk or in the grass and just listen.

Sometimes I would go alone, other times I would invite a few friends, who enjoyed music as much as I do. They would sneak a few beers out of their refrigerator at home, pack it in a cooler underneath soda and ice then we would have our own party, with live music. It was kick-ass. Great times and awesome fucking memories.

It was also an escape from my shitty existence of a life. Although if I had known that years later I would be where I am now, life would have been so much easier. I have reached every career milestone I have set for myself, for the band. Now a days, it seems like I'm waiting to find that one fucking kid, the same kid I once was with nothing to lose. Hopping fences to hear us. To see us play. That would make our career, my career.

Returning to my stalkerish peeping, I spot a girl in the far back row but she's too far away to make out everything. I can see that she's just sitting there, with an air of righteousness. Her nose upturned in the air. She clearly doesn't want to be here. I laugh aloud. Wait until we hit the stage, and let's see if I can change her attitude around.

It's not common for people like her to be at a concert of ours because usually you have to pay for a ticket, and why would you pay for a ticket to a concert of a band you don't even like ? I know exactly how I'll change her outlook. It works like a charm every damn time. I glance at my watch, twenty minutes until show time. Might as well head back to the band. It's time to rock this fucking house.

I walk into our makeshift dressing room; Jason is pacing back and forth while taking a shot of Jameson. The guy gets stage fright, even after eight years, guess that's also why he stays behind those drums. "Listen up boys. Jason - you cool it. We've got ourselves one of those uppity bitches in the audience. You know what that means." I say eyeing each one of the guys; they all nod their heads knowing exactly what our plan will be. "We need to break her yeah?"

"Hell Yeah!" They yell. We've made it this fucking far, if you're going to attend our fucking concert then you damn well better enjoy it. Jason offers me a shot, and I down it. The fire lights a way straight to my inner core.   A few more shots and then we'll be fucking ready.

We make our way to the stage; the lights down low. We can barely see so I know the audience can't see shit. They have no idea that we are less than a foot away. As I grab my guitar, I look to the right of me, making sure Zepp and Liam are ready, glancing over my shoulder, Jason nods, then to my left Gage on Bass winks provocatively, that perverted bastard.

We're ready.

One lone light shines down on us. Everyone becomes silent for one small moment, and then. Then they fucking scream. I walk up to the microphone stand, glide my hand into place and pull it to me like a woman's slender neck, ready to receive my kiss. I set my lips very close to the microphone and breathe out.

"What the fuck is up BOSTON!!!!" I scream. Random words are all yelled back in our direction.

"Do you want to fucking party with us?" Everyone in the audience replies back in the loudest scream.

"Fuck yeah!" Then, Zepp, Gage, and Liam all synchronize, playing into rhythm. Jason starts beating the drums like a fucking god. And I, I sing the fucking song.

"As I lay dying, I think about the memories the memories of yesterday..." I close my eyes letting the music take over me. It washes throughout my veins. The energy and the emotion in the music that my boys are putting out is unexplainable. The crowd is drinking it up, and then retching it. Throwing it back to us.

Fans are body surfing throughout this fucking place, trying to get even closer to us. Security strategically placed in front of the stage are shoving people back in droves. I fucking grin; I love this shit. Moving across the stage, working every angle, my eyes zoom all the way to the back row dead center and this bitch is the only one unfazed in this entire fucking room.

She's unimpressed. Our first song is almost over; I cock my head backwards and glance at the guys. They know it's time, usually I choose wait until the middle of our set, but everyone except for Jason has worked this stage. They can see how unaffected this girl is. I pace while Gage and Zepp do a fade out. Ending the song.

I strut back to the middle of the stage, place the microphone back in the stand, point my right finger at her and say "Honey?" her head turns to me, eyes wide.

Then glances around her. She's unsure I'm speaking to her "Yes. You." I state. Matter-of -factly.

"Why don't you get your ass up here on my stage?" I yell, shooting daggers at her.

I have to make sure she understands that I'm not fucking joking; I don't invite just anybody onto our stage. The crowd is going fucking wild, heads turned around to see whom I am talking about. By their reactions, they want to see me make an example of her, their hungry for it.

A few people get loose of the pit; they start walking to the back of the auditorium. They're planning on bringing her to me; I can tell. Like bringing a pig to slaughter. They the farmhands, wanting to eat it all up.

Some are screaming out "Who the fuck is she?"

Like I must know this superior broad that this is part of the show. Soon. Minutes actually, they will be assured it most certainly is not.

CHAPTER FIVE

Natalie

 *s I lay dying..."*

I hear his throaty aggressive rasp. It's sexy as hell and all man. My mind does not want to be attracted to this voice. My body has other plans and my ears are taking it all in. This man can sing. Enjoy his songs, I do not. But god damn I could listen to his voice A-Cappella all night.

If I mentioned one word about this to Layla, she would never let me live it down. I am not a fan of change, and I would never voluntarily listen to this band. I've heard a few of their songs on the radio. Enough to remember who it was and then change the station. Not without Layla displaying those pouty eyes trying to beg me to keep it there.

Whoever said that every band sounds the same live as they do on their albums, are liars. I have never heard an artist sound so much better live on stage, then they do on their songs.

His voice is knocking me down, breaking my musical barriers. Then he opens his mouth to speak rather than sing, and slowly ruins every thought I just had.

"Honey?" I hear, rather than see him. It would be pitch black in here if it weren't for one solo light. That's currently shining on me. I look around, hoping, praying.

Surely, he isn't talking to me.

Anyone else but me.

"Yes, you" he yells.

The lights come on, and he's staring right at me. I stare back. He is pissed. What could I have possibly done, to piss of a complete stranger so much?

"Why don't you get your ass up here on stage?" Not asking, but demanding.

I see a few people walking toward me, his self-appointed minions. I look behind me, to the door. Maybe, just maybe I could make it out before they reached me. I look back to the crowd; Layla is on the outside barrier of people. Still with Benjamin. Her eyes currently pleading with me to just do as asked. She wants me to go.

Fight or flight.

I choose fight. No one is carrying me; I'll walk willingly. I put my feet down flat on the floor and stand up. Looking him in the eye, not to show submission, but to show that I am an equal. Making my way to the stage the crowd of people part a path for me to walk through. I feel eyes on me. Looking up to confirm whom they belong to. It was as I thought. Steele. Glaring holes right through me. A tight smirk playing upon his face. What game is he playing? I ponder maybe this is part of their show. Randomly calling out women from the audience.

So I walk slower. He can wait on me.

I study his face. He is what I would consider beautiful.

My heart is pounding erratically. He runs his hand through his jet black hair. It's falling down in cascading waves slightly shading his eyes.   Eyes that I can partially see, staring back at me. A color so magnificent, the ocean blue, but obviously laced with pain, an emotion so intense I can almost feel it pouring out of him and embracing me. With an overwhelming sensation, my breath hitches.

I reach the stairs; one step closer to confronting this brooding stranger. I walk up the steps one at a time. As slowly as possible. He reaches his hand out; I reluctantly grasp it and let him pull me up. Stumbling I fall into him, he catches my fall, my chest landing against his. I can feel he is as affected as I am by this.

His heart is pounding, slowly matching the rhythm of my own. Calm the fuck down Nat, I tell myself.

Correcting myself, standing upright quickly, face reddening. I look behind me and realize that I had forgotten the large mass of people that are also witnessing my humiliation not only at falling into his embrace, but that I was ordered to stand upon this stage. I glance at the band with a help me look. They do not seem surprised that I was called up here, they know exactly what's about to happen.

This gorgeous specimen of a man interferes in my space, grabs my hand, then leans his head into the side of my face and whispers in my ear "About time you came up here, I'm Steele. You know most women would have ran up here."

I take a step back withdrawing my hand from his. Bewildered and angered by his presumptuous tone that I should be honored to stand next to him. I look around, searching for someone who isn't Okay with this. But everyone, including my best friend is begging, pleading for something to happen.

Well Fuck it. I'll give them what they want; then I'm fucking gone. I stare at Steele, right into his torment filled eyes, and say, "What do you want?"

He and I are the only ones who can hear what is being said. Thank God.

"You obviously weren't enjoying the show, so I thought I would make yah part of it Minx."

"Tell me, Steele," I hiss. "How did you figure that my being up here is going to make me enjoy your show?"

"Well Honey, it's going to work, because you're going to be singing a song with me." He states with confidence.

"You're delusional. Lyrics? I don't know one word to any of your fucking songs." I say hysterically.

This guy is fucking crazy. He starts laughing, putting his right arm over his stomach, bent over gasping for breath because he finds my predicament so hilarious.

"I don't think this is funny."

What seems like minutes later, he stands upright and wipes the smile off his face. Replacing it with a no nonsense, downright dangerous glare.

"Now, why are you going to lie to me like that? I highly doubt you haven't heard any of our songs, for fuck sakes you are going to college for music. Let's get this fucking moving. You're singing. With me."

"What song?" I ask resigning myself to this; if I just sing this goddamn song then I can leave.

"Used by you." He smirks.

What a bastard.

"I'm not singing that song with you, it's about cheapening the meaning of love, and degradation of women. An example of everything I despise in mainstream music. No, I'm not going to fucking do it." I snarl.

"Ha! So you do know one of our songs!" He exclaims, quite happily it seems.

I'm defeated; I just want to get this done and over with. This is probably the only song I know well enough to attempt singing, and as soon as I do this, I won't have to see him again. At this moment, leaving is all I want to do. The only reason I am still standing right here on this stage. Is because I am about to knock him on his smug ass.

Unbeknownst to him I can sing, I've been compared to some of the best female voices of all time.

"Well let's get this moving." I say.

He turns to the band members; they all take their place. Unfortunately, Steele and I have to share a microphone. The song starts with the drummer hammering on the snare and bass drum. The bassist and guitarists both start in on the same cue. Making this earth enchanting rhythm, almost hypnotizing. The stage is vibrating beneath my feet. Shaking me to my core.

Looking into Steele's eyes and he into mine and together start to sing every verse harmonizing.

"When I first met you, you were fucking crazy

Maybe that's why your pussy didn't faze me

So used and abused

Unconscious and boozed

Sharing yourself with every-one

You couldn't make me cum

Clothes tattered and torn

You were screaming out for more..."

The song ends. I scan the audience, seeing that they are pleased. I run. Down the stairs of the stage, out the auditorium. Out of the college. I run. I keep running until I am gasping for air.

My ribs are screaming out in pain, but I don't want to stop. Not until I am home where I can think about what the hell just happened and the consequences of my running away. So I keep going. For over five miles, I run as if the grim reaper himself were chasing me claiming me for death. As soon as I get home, I race to my bedroom and lock my door.

No doubts as to whether or not Layla is going to want to discuss this. I know I sure as hell don't want to. I sit on my bed and place my head between my knees breathing in and out. I can feel a panic attack coming on. The slight dizziness in my head, the drink I had earlier fighting its way out, with every muscle in my body tensing.

This point in the anxiety game is when every single one of my fears lace together and run amuck in my head. I feel as if I am held hostage there having to bear witness to every possible worse scenario that could ever conceivably happen to ones I love, ever loved or even myself. My fears, they bridge forming one piece. Pain and death. I'm forever fighting to keep people out, because, at any moment, anyone can die from anything, and I never want to feel that pain ever again.

My breath stolen from my lungs, and my heart breaking into a million pieces. I was the one left alive, knowing I would trade my life for theirs. But it's impossible.

Death is final. There is nothing I can do to change it now.

It's been years, and I still feel that void that will never fill. I'm frozen. Nothing and no one can ever relieve the emptiness inside of my heart. For the attack to subside sooner, I have to let the reins loose, and my battle to maintain control down to a minimum. I just have to go with it. Face it. And eventually everything will be all right. My mantra, I keep telling myself repeatedly. It will be all right. One day, I will get over this. These feelings will not have a hold over me. Maybe then, I can let someone in. Slowly, my thoughts became my own, and any fears I had were thrown to the back of my subconscious.

The door slams! I jerked my head out of my lap. Who in the hell is that? I ask myself. I run out into the living room and see Layla and Benjamin.

"As your best friend I'm going to ask, are you all right?" Layla says in a controlled manner while Benjamin acts as if he would rather anywhere else in the world at the precise moment.

"Yeah, I'm fine. I was just full of nerves and didn't want to be ambushed by all of the crazy fans, yah know."

"Yeah, YEAH! Nat I completely understand how you fucked this up for YOU, for US. Ryan Fucking Steele asked you. YOU! To come up onto his stage, and what do you do? You hightail it out of there before he could get your name, let alone speak to you." She yells punctuating each and every word.

I underestimated her anger.

"I hope your joking right now Layla. I mean you are joking right?" A hint of anger lacing my voice.

"I'm not playing." Layla says annoyed.

"I know you wanted me to go up there, you were practically begging me with your eyes. But I was humiliated, he did it on purpose." Snapping back.

"You didn't hear our conversation. He was taunting me; he was making an example out of me because I wasn't enjoying their god damn show." At this point, I am yelling.

"It doesn't matter. What matters is you could have learned from a legend, his entire empire is made up of THE BEST in this business. Instead, you have to fuck up every single good thing you have coming your way."

Instantly I retort, "It wasn't what..."

She cuts me off. "I don't want to hear it. I'm done discussing this. I'm going out with Benjamin. I won't be home until Monday for class. We just came back so I could grab a change of clothes. Think about what I said."

And with that she just walks away. I can't even speak. Layla and I never argue; we may disagree on a few things here and there as they come up. Ultimately though, we always just let the other be. We've never fought about each other's actions or choices. Flabbergasted, I decide to hide out in my room until they leave.

CHAPTER SIX

Steele

$\mathcal{W}$e finish our set thanking everyone for entering the contest- a contest that the band nor I approved of or was even aware that our tour manager Mel had allowed us to be entered in. I storm off backstage, the guys following.

Shocked. That's the only way I can describe what I'm feeling. I reenter our dressing room. Before I can even speak, Jason does. "The princess you had on stage was something else Ryan, she has some fight in her. It's not a surprise she stuck out to you in that mob of fans."

"What do you mean it's not a surprise that she caught my attention?" I question, wondering what he could be implying.

"Cool it man, all I'm saying is that the chick was easily the most unapproachable in that entire horde. Also, she was easily the sexiest." He says almost laughing.

"Yeah well it didn't go exactly how I had planned. She ran dude; fucking ran."

At that precise moment, a female walks in interrupting our conversation. She introduces herself to Jason first, then Gage, Zepp and Liam, then me.

"I'm Layla," she says, in a smooth seductive tone.

"Uh, Hi Layla and what may I do for you?" I say with a suggestive wink. This girl is fucking hot; thing is she knows it. I'm unsure if this is a good thing or a bad thing with her.

"Oh no, baby, it's not what you can do for me but what I can do for you. You see that hot little thing you were just singing with on stage, well I know her name. Am I wrong in assuming you might want to know it too?" She says sure of herself.

I look around at the guys; curiosity laid out over their faces. They want to know as bad as I do who this girl is. The one- the only person we've come across that's remained unflustered, almost offended by our music. I mask my features, needing to remain calm, cool and collected. I don't want any of them to really see how interested I am; I want to teach this little girl a lesson or two.

No one runs from me.

"Sure. So what's her name and who is she to you. I mean she has to be somebody if you would risk sneaking past security to get in here. Am I right?" I say back sounding uninterested.

"One, she's my best friend. Two, if you hurt with her I will come after you." She says threateningly. "And three, her name is Natalie. Natalie Wright."

It's clear this girl means something to her, but I will heed to her warning. "You have nothing to worry about; I don't plan on seeking her out. She's a college kid for Christ sakes. Nothing special." She flinches as if I cut her.

"Security" I yell.

"Will you help this kind young woman find her way out?"

Dee offers her his hand, and she reluctantly takes it, glancing back she says, "Remember what I said? Don't hurt her." And with that she disappears from my view.

"Drinks. Now. This is our last few days off consecutively so let's enjoy it. Also, is that bet still on?" Gage walks over five bottles of Whiskey in hand, no need for those girly shot glasses. When we drink, it's to get fucked up.

Zepp starts laughing, "Hell Yeah, that bets still on, let the battle begin."

And with that we all smack our bottles together and drink until we can't handle the burn anymore.

I wake up to the light streaming through the windows. When I open my eyes, pain shoots straight to my head. Fucking alcohol, I always seem to forget why I choose to stop drinking. Alas, the morning after never fails to remind me exactly how shitty it really is.

At that moment, I realize I have to piss in a bad way, but I cannot get up. I am pinned by arms and legs at least two sets of each. This is going to take some time. Slowly, one by one I remove said limbs. Careful not to wake the owners, creeping across the bed I glance at the naked beauties. Smiling because at least while drunk I still had a high set of standards.

I shimmy my ass down the bed, not wanting to wake these girls. Wanting to escape cleanly and free, no begging for a commitment or a phone number or even my address. It gets old and frankly, it's quite pathetic.

A woman is worth one night only to me, after that I'm good. Why ruin a sexually adventurous experience? I creep to the bathroom take a piss then go on searching for my clothes, my shirt covering a lampshade. My jeans on the headboard of the bed my socks and shoes in front of the door. I throw them on and run out of the door.

As I shut the door, I realize by looking down the hallway, I must have taken the girls back to the same hotel were staying in. Well that makes it a whole hell of a lot easier. At this moment, all I want is a cigarette, hot shower and a cup of coffee and a side of aspirin. Maybe then the hangover will subside enough to get through these damn interviews today. That reminds me, I have yet to get Mel's input on exactly what I should be looking for.

Putting the keycard in my hotel room door. I overhear a girl.

"Thank you so much for last night baby; I left my number on your night stand .Call me."

I turn around and witness probably one of the best walk of shames I have ever seen. This woman's hair is stiff as a board pointing in every direction, mascara running around her eyes as if she is a raccoon and her lipstick smeared all the way to her ear. I have everything I can do not to laugh aloud. What a surprise that must have been opening your eyes up to that sight.

As soon as she is out of earshot, I burst out laughing barely catching my breath, "Oh shut the hell up already would you? My count: one" Gage states.

When I manage to catch my bearings I stand up straight, look him in the eye mischievously and say "My count: two" and with that I turn my heel and walk into my room.

I let my door shut itself, and strip my clothes from yesterday off. Placing an order with room service, I order an entire breakfast tray of fruit and pastries. Knowing that the guys will be knocking at my door by the time I am out of the shower and dressed. Its tradition, the night after a show. We regroup in the morning.

Communication is one of the reasons we have made it to the top, when you are in a five person rock group you always have to maintain that open line.

Hanging up with the hotels kitchen, I walk into the bathroom and start a steaming hot shower.

I didn't even bother placing my hand under the rain shower of water to check the temperature. I just jump under the stream, back facing the showerhead. I run my hands through my hair, exhaling everything I have been holding in the past two days. Pissed off at Mel, Pissed off at that strange female.

Grabbing the hotel branded shampoo, I squirt a dollop into my hand and sniff, flowers. How fitting, to smell of a girl. Fuck it. I start scrubbing it into my scalp, once my head in covered in a soapy lather I rinse. Taking the paper covered bar of soap the size of a matchbook the hotel again provided so freely, I rip the paper wrapper off and cup it in my hand   running it all over my body, turning around, so I face the shower head I close my eyes and allow myself to go back to last night.

She looked so haunted. Disturbed even. There was a turbulence of emotions in her murky brown eyes thorough out entire interaction. Part of me almost felt bad for what I was going to do to her. What I attempted to do anyways. I almost backed out as she made her way, but her eyes lied about her strength. She fought back, which of course makes me all the more curious.

I should just let it go and move on. We're only here for a few more days. What could I possibly learn about her? If I leave this hotel, I will be lucky not to have a horde of people following me. One of the downfalls? No privacy. Ever. So without privacy

I'm not able to go around asking questions about her. If one sneaky press affiliate or groupie heard, I was asking around about a random female, news headlines would make the front page. Claiming I possibly knocked someone up or some other imaginative tale.

Deciding my skin is as clean as it's going to get. I turn the shower off, step out take the towel off the fancy towel rack and dry my body off. I strut out of the bathroom and grab my luggage bag out of the closet, I never unpack. I yank out a pair of blue Calvin Klein boxer briefs my favorite, diesel jeans, and a t-shirt. Smoke time. Stopping in front of the mirror on my way out I throw my hands through my hair, messing it up just a little bit. Perfect.

Grabbing my cigarettes and lighter I leave my room and make my way down to the concierge desk, asking the woman behind it if there is a discreet smoking spot. She points me in the right direction and I head outside. I don't smoke a lot, with a profession of lead singer I have to be careful not to ruin my vocal chords. Nicotine, I can't forget about, I've tried kicking the habit. It isn't going to happen so I just cut down, a few a day to get me through.

Stepping through the door, it's hot as a bitch out; even with the wind blowing in from the harbor it doesn't make the heat any more bearable. Thank god for Air conditioner. Originally born down south, you'd think I was accustom to handle it. Nope. Exhaling my cloud of smoke, I take a look around. She sent me to the roof, its abandoned all but a couple of beat up plastic chairs, the ones you buy at Walmart for ten bucks you sit in it and if you make one wrong move the leg snaps off. I choose to stay standing, not taking a chance of falling on my ass.

Thinking I should call Mel before breakfast with the guys, I take my cell out and speed dial his number putting the speaker to my ear. "You still pissed off?" He says wearily.

"Not as pissed as I was two days ago, I wasn't calling to chew you out again, even though I really fucking want to. Just don't throw shit on me like that again. You know our tour starts in a few days. The guys were saying goodbye to their families and you took that away. You're lucky they agreed to come along.

Anyway, who am I interviewing and what is going to be their job?" I ask, chewing on my lip as a reminder to just shut my mouth and not jump down his throat.

"They are interns; literally all we have to pay for is accommodations and meals. They work for free, learning whatever they can on the way. It's not up to me what you're looking for. It's ultimately the bands choice. Berklee is a huge school; everyone is getting a degree under music. You have the pick of the litter here. Take advantage of it. I have a professor that will help accommodate you and set you up with interviews. He will give you and the guys transcripts you might have an interest in taking a look over." He explains.

"That's all?" I ask with a slight annoyed laugh, not even slightly amused.

"Don't sound so interested, remember when I found you guys all playing in that hole in the wall bar. You had all you could do not to beg me to take you on; I took a chance. Pay it forward Ryan. This school has the cream of the crop. These kids have to work their asses off. If they don't, they don't stay past the next semester." He says defending students he has never met.

"All right, just give me this teacher's name and where I can locate him, I'll let the guys know our plan for the day when we meet up for grub." He then proceeds to tell me what building I will find Professor Roberts in.

I hang up, put my smoke out and throw it in the ashtray then make my way back to my room where I am sure the guys have already made their way to and are stuffing their faces.

They better have saved me a fucking cup of coffee. As I near my door, I can overhear them, yup as I figured. It really is a bad idea, handing each other's room keys out. It has its upsides, also its downfalls.

I enter and in unionism all I hear is "TWO? Really two fucking girls?" I laugh, must be I am already in the lead.

Serves them right, bringing this wager on, I'm going to have to come up with a much more creatively humiliating thing for these losers to do this time when I beat them. A way to start off tour with a fucking bang.

"Come on guys, you've all had two or more at once, don't act so innocent. In fact, I'm pretty sure Gage here has had four women at once. I walked in on it, in MY hotel room at that," I remind them.

"Don't forget, you told me that night you wouldn't be back and I didn't want them to know which room I was in. Plus one of the girls did offer to suck your dick, to make up for your sour ass mood." He says defensively.

"If you remember right, I was only in a sour mood because I had just outrun a crazy obsessed fan-girl, who didn't know the meaning of No." At that we all start laughing. I remember that morning clearly.

I decided to join this after-party, big fucking mistake there. I wanted a night of normalcy. Never again. Lesson definitely learned. This hot piece of ass, walked right up to me, yanked me into a bedroom, got on her knees and started unbuckling my jeans. Who in the fuck was I to say no? A blowjob, I will take any-day. I wasn't going to stop her; I returned the favor with a rough fucking.

I thought she had passed out. I went to sneak out, and she jumped out of bed talking about fucking marriage. This girl was defiantly not a virgin, and I'm not marrying anyone. When I made that clear, she went psycho crazy, throwing shit at me and crying. I've never gotten dressed so fast and then I booked it out of there.

She took off behind me, naked. Truth be known that's the last time I partied in Houston.

A man's one-night stand nightmare. This bitch was fucking crazy, the entire time I was running from this nut job I kept thinking where the fuck are the police. This one should be locked up; I pity the next person she involves in her life sexually. It was certainly the last thing I had expected to happen, and then that last statement became false, as I entered MY hotel room.

There is Gage, completely fucking naked, his penis at full staff two woman sharing it with their mouths while another two women are on the side pleasing each other. On my bed.

"What in the fuck is this Gage?" I practically scream, reaching my boiling point because of the crazy I was just running from.

"Want to join? There is more than enough pussy to go around." I raised my eyebrow, seriously considering it, but in the end deciding that I'll sit this one out.

Just wanting to find a bed to crawl into and sleep for the next twelve hours. As I was exiting the room one of the girls who had just been laying her saliva on Gages' cock offered to take care of mine, I declined and left.

"So down to business." I say snapping out of the past, not that they noticed because they were eating every bit of food I had ordered.

"We have to make a visit to campus, we'll probably be there for most of the day interviewing for interns. Mel says it's a must. Our recording label signed a contract with the contest organization. Winning included a performance and an intern for the summer." I tell them, wondering if they're as pissed off as I am about it.

"Why not?" Zepp says.

"The way I see it, our team is going to help someone learn the trade, it only seems fitting they learn from the mother-fucking best. We will have to filter out the applicants, see if there being true or want to just tour with us. Let's go for it."

Everyone else agrees. Seems I'm the only one feeling put out over this.

"Let's go find this Professor then."

Making sure I grab another cup of coffee before we leave. Exiting the hotel, our limousine is already there waiting on us. Already aware of where we are headed, Pat opens our doors, and we climb in, I demanding to sit on the outside since I am the only one who smokes. I light up, rolling the window down as far as it will go. Guess I'm going to be smoking a lot more than usual today. Only way to calm my nerves a bit.

My patience has been trying since Mel called me three days ago and told me about this shit. I am not a fan of surprises. I plan, and I control everything around me. I also have the final say on anything concerned with the band, this not solely my decision. The guys know I have nothing but our best interest in mind, and that I am a man willing to make it happen. I do not compromise or bend to anyone's will. You want us; then you give in to our demands.

Pat opens my door first. I get out, and he informs me that the red brick building about one hundred feet from us is where we will find the one and only Professor Roberts and also where every possible intern is waiting for an interview. Over eighty he says. I grimace; it's going to be a long fucking day...

I turn to the guys and explain what Pat just said. Exciting interest laid upon all of their faces. Fucking Joy. Entering the building there's a desk located just before me with a pretty little thing sitting there in a rolling chair feet up legs crossed and filing her nails.

"Professor Roberts" I ask for.

Without hesitation, nor looking up to welcome us she says "Down the hall about thirty feet, first door on your left and have a nice day."

With that, we walk right by. College kids. I think, shaking my head. This school is for the privileged. Pat also informed me of that great detail. Even more of a reason for me to despise my future intern. Meeting the Professors door, I knock. After the first pound of my fist, the door opens. An eccentric old man answers the door, smiles and clasps his hands together. "How wonderful you are all here!" He exclaims.

Sensing the tension in the air, he ignores it and keeps going "I have every student's file who applied right here." Pointing at his desk to a mound of paperwork stacked upon it. "They are all in order, you just pull the first file from the top and so on, and I also made a list. You can leave comments if you like. These kids are so excited. Would you like to start now?" He asks.

"Sure" we all agree. He points to a table with five chairs on one side and one singular chair on the other. He tells us he will give us a few minutes with each file before sending the person in so we can go over their transcripts.

Closing the door, he says, "You will find we only educate the most ambitious students."

I take a seat, Zepp, Liam, Gage and Jason joining me.

"So who wants to go over our first file, we can take turns being the speaker and asking questions. Sound good?" They agree, and Jason agrees to be the first. "Rundown, our first applicant enrolled in a four year degree, wants to be a sound engineer. Two years under his belt." With that were ready for our first candidate.

In walks a kid, couldn't be older than nineteen, buzz cut and in a suit. I can see the sweat running down his temple; he's nervous as hell. Hoping he doesn't vomit all over my hand while I offer him my hand in a shake, introducing myself.

"Ryan, how are yah feeling today?"

He swallows and with a trembling voice, he replies. "Gg-rreatt. Namm-es Sssccchh-uyler." He looks embarrassed over his stutter, quickly we all act as if we didn't notice.

"Well Schuyler were just going to ask you a couple of questions and then we well set yah free, all right? Tell me what makes you so interested in spending your summer with us on tour?"

He wipes his head with his forearm.

"You guys are just my favorite band and I have to get out there sometime, somehow, someway. I have two years left and if I am able to do this I will receive extra credit. Touring with a number one band will only make my resume look better." He says with unexpected confidence. I accept his answer and allow the guys to ask the rest of their questions.

I run my fingers in my hair, leaving them to support my head. I zone out. Thinking about the night our lives changed forever. We had been playing together for about a year. Liam had gotten us a gig in some washed up bar in Manhattan. Really just trying to put a few dollars in our pockets for gas and food to hit the next stop. We played music and did a show for shit pay, because we loved it. Some days I think if I could go back, I would. Just to be able to revel in the experience still unknown. We were on our last song, when I noticed a suit sitting in the back right corner. He was out of place, definitely not belonging in an establishment such as this.

Trusting my gut feeling, I pushed every fiber of myself into that damn song. A song we still preform at every one of our concerts. After the show he approached us, Mel was his name, and he had been looking for a rock band to sign. He wanted us to come into the office, talk some figures and test us out in the studio. He would then send our single to a few radio stations, see what the feedback was and that would be the deciding factor if we were offered a contract or not.

I wasn't a fucking fool. They supplied us with one of the shittiest songs. Not letting us do our own shit, I demanded they sign us, or we walk. Before releasing that previously recorded single. They refused, so we walked. The guys were hesitant; we shared a two bedroom apartment in Brooklyn and our income was negative. Asking for their trust, I knew what I was doing and sure enough.

Mel called less than three days later "Call an entertainment lawyer", he had said. On the 28th of February in 2007, our lives were forever changed.

It was then; I had an epiphany. A triumphant laugh escaped me, interrupting Gage finishing up with our candidate. Said intern excused himself and shut the door. Then the guys faced me all eyes full of questions. "So I have an amazing fucking idea that will help solve our interview dilemma. I don't want to be here all day, nor do you guys. We could use the next couple days to chill. Then hit the road." I tell them.

"Were listening," Zepp says.

"Here it is that girl from last night" the anguished and broken one I finish to myself.

"And...." impatiently Gage replies.

"She could be our intern, I could tell the Professor we want her, we know her name after all. She is obviously majoring in music, or she wouldn't be here. Everyone is required to do a summer internship to get their degree, or so Pat informed me."

"Pretty sure that the princess has no interest in our band, or our music let alone touring with us Ryan. Entertain me, how would you coax her into this?" Gage points out.

Fuck. I only suggested this with malicious intent; I want to break her. I have to. Since last night. She has been popping into my head, and I don't like it, not one bit. I want her out! The way I see it the sooner I break this privileged bitch, the sooner she disappears in my head. The guys would be pissed though. If they knew that I didn't truly want to help her, only wanting her to be our intern to break her and nothing more.

But it's not hurting someone physically. And this girl, this golden haired beauty, I just want to hurt her emotionally. I want to slice deep into her soul with my words. Make her see that every song has to be heard, every feeling felt. I just want her to fucking take it in. With that last thought, I plead my case to the guys "If she doesn't want to, we could talk to the Professor. Maybe bribe him with a donation. He's the only one who could make this happen."

The guys all nod their heads, going along with me. "Just hope you know what you're doing man, I know you want to break her. But just think, she's going to be with us for the next two and a half months, how bad do you want to rock her fucking world?" Gage says, always insightful. Of course, I deny what he is implying; assuring him I know what I'm getting myself into.

I step outside, waiting for the Professor to come back with the next student. About three minutes later he appears an obvious groupie on his side. No way is this girl an excelling talent. I show her in and then shut the door, staying outside of the office. I ask Professor Roberts if there is somewhere we can go to talk privately. He starts wringing his hands nervously.

He shows me to a much smaller office, then the one I was just in. I shut the door and proceed to kissing this man's ass. "I see; you guys have a really nice set up here, and the bands who opened for us last night. I heard some raw talent...anyway, I had an idea. There is this student, from last night. She is whom we want as an intern. We would also make a twenty-five thousand donation to your department." I said with a smile. Careful not to say that he would only get the donation if I was guaranteed Natalie would take on the internship.

Manipulation. Anyone who works at a school like this thrives off donations for their departments. At first he looks offended because I even attempted to bribe him. It was well played because I can also see the resignation in his eyes. He will accept.

With a shaky voice, "What is her name?" he asks.

"Natalie Wright" I state.

"She won't go, she would never voluntarily intern for your band."

Not acceptable.

I violate his area, step in close, stare him in the eyes and almost in a whisper I regretfully threaten "Make it happen, do whatever you have to. I don't care; she is going, and you will make sure of it." With that, I turned around and left the office slamming the door behind me.

Fuck. I hope he doesn't go around telling people, what I just did qualified as a form of blackmail.

CHAPTER SEVEN

Natalie

$\mathcal{F}$our days later, after the argument with Layla, I find myself packing. She and I still haven't spoken. I hope that she comes home before I have to leave. I would hate to not be able to say goodbye, even if shit is a little tense between us.

Going through all of my drawers deciding what I will need for the next two months, I think about exactly how I ended up in this predicament. No choice but to go, praying summer flies.

Monday morning in class Professor Roberts asked if I could stay after so he could talk to me. I was on pins and needles the entire class, wondering what he could possibly have to say. I am an excellent student, always holding an A or above average. Using my free time valuably, doing school work or extra credit. As class is dismissed, I lingered behind.

Walking down the steps, I see Professor glance at me nervously. This was only raising my anxiety a notch further. As the last student leaves, he shuts the door behind them.

"Natalie. There was something I needed to discuss with you. Since this is the ending to your second year, it's mandatory that you intern with an artist and at a recording studio. You were given many choices and looking through your transcripts I see that you didn't apply anywhere." He says rambling.

This piqued my curiosity. He has had numerous occurrences where he had an opportunity to bring this to my attention. Why wait until now?

"I'm sorry Professor I wasn't aware it was mandatory that I intern this year, I thought it was for my third and fourth year. What does this mean for me then if I do not have a position interning?" I ask nervously.

"It would mean that you would fail this semester. Thus having to retake these courses in the fall. Knowing you wouldn't want to risk failing I could pull a few strings and set you up with a band. It's only for two months, and you will be on tour with them. It would benefit you greatly Natalie."

I huff, really left with no other option.

"I'll do it but it's only because I don't have a choice. So who am I interning with?"

Hindsight is always twenty-twenty. Had I known that Steele's Army or Ryan fucking Steele, whatever the hell his name is, was my only option I would have told Professor Roberts to shove it up his ass. I should have seen this coming. Remembering now that Layla mentioned they were offering an internship as part of the contest. I should have known. I also should have realized how the Professor was playing me, like a god damn violin.

"Don't worry about who Miss Wright. Seize the opportunity. You need to do this, and it will be excellent for you. You'll be working side by side with some of the greats." He's trying to reassure me.

While handing me a piece of paper, he says, "I wrote down where the tour bus will be leaving from. Be there Friday at nine A.M. precisely. They will leave without you if you aren't there. Also, I suggest packing light, there's only so much room." With that, he grabbed his suitcase and left me with my mouth still agape.

How did this happen?

Back to reality, Layla still isn't home. Instead of packing last night, I chose to lay in bed all night, reveling in the comfortableness of it, the security of the life I have now. Assisting a musician on tour has been my career goal for as long as I can remember. It's also way out of my comfort zone; I enjoy my privacy, my showers, and my walks. On tour, my shower will be taken in a tiny compartment, barely any room to lift your arms to scrub your hair.

The only walks I will be taking is backstage, and my privacy will be nonexistent. My bed will be a bunk over another located in a niche in the wall. So I spent last night spoiling myself in what I had. Of course that also meant I had to wake up, and six am, so I could enjoy my shower one last time for the next two months. Then pack, then hopefully say goodbye to Layla's and walk over to the Ritz.

I lay my suitcase on the bed. Opening my drawers just tossing in underwear, bras, t-shirts, jeans. Deciding I should have at least one professional outfit on hand, I take my plain black dress out of my closet and a pair of red wedges. Stuffing that in my suitcase as well, I go to the kitchen and grab three plastic gallon sized storage bags to put my bathroom necessities in. My toothbrush, toothpaste, mouthwash, shampoo and conditioner, bath poof, body wash, and hairbrush. I zip my luggage bag, throw a pair of flip flops in the outer pocket , wiping my hair from my face, glancing around my room checking to see if I missed anything I might want.

In my purse, I already have my cellphone and charger. The two things I could not live without. Looking at my bed, I see my parents' picture in a frame on my nightstand. I walk over to it pick it up, and remove the picture out of the frame. I'll keep that in my bunk with me .I have to take a piece of them with me. I wheel my bag to the front door. As I take my cellphone out of my purse to call a cab. I see Layla walking through the front door. Glad to see her, I hang up just so I can have one uninterrupted moment to let her know what's going on. I give her the short story. Telling her that I would rather spend the summer with her and how I have no choice doing this internship. Being the best friend that she is, she understands and offers to drive me to the hotel that the bus is leaving from just so we could have a few more minutes together.

To outsiders it might seem odd that we are so close. We don't go around explaining how our friendship is so much more. Its sisterhood. She was there throughout my loss. It was her loss also. She remained strong for me. She carried me when I needed her it most through life and even though she put my feet on the ground; she still has my hand. She's fought my demons with me, sometimes without my help. She has always supported me and has remained my closest friend throughout it all. I love her, and she is the only family that I have left.

On the way to the bus, I tell her to call me when she can and that I will send her many pictures and texts updating her throughout my day. It will be as if we are spending the summer together. She tells me that once I find out the exact tour schedule I should send it to her. Suggesting to meet up with me at a few of the shows, hoping we stay in one city more than a day and spend the day together if the itinerary allows.

"You have got to be fucking kidding me!" I squeal, causing Layla to slam on the brakes. I don't have to say a word. She knows exactly why I'm freaking. The tour busses, two actually, are pulled right up to the curb of the sidewalk. Surrounding a gorgeous upscale hotel pushing the lock button on the door handle, I lock Layla and myself in the car.

"You are aware I have the keys Nat? Also I have the same buttons on my door handle as well." She says smiling.

"Well I can tell you are happy about this. Did you plan this? I can't believe this." I say rolling my eyes.

"Nat, how would I have been able to arrange this, I don't have that kind of power. Hell they kicked me out of their dressing room when I offered to help them." She smacks her hand over her lips, realizing what she just let slip.

"What do you mean you offered to help them? Tell me how Layla, how?" I say now highly aggravated.

"I just told them your name I promise. That's all. Steele didn't even look impressed. He had no interest discussing you at all. So I doubt this was something that was planned. Professor Roberts probably pulled a few strings like he said. You can't back out now Nat. You don't want to fail this year, or do you?" She asks, already knowing the answer.

"I'll text you the tour stops and pop your trunk please." I say while unlocking the door and getting out.

"Nat, please don't leave like this. Give me a hug and promise me you're not mad at me." She pleads.

I walk around to the trunk, grab my luggage, and then walk to the driver's side window. Reaching my arm in through the open window to pull her into a half hug. "I love yah, I'm not mad and I will get call you as soon as I can." With that, I walk away to my summer of torture.

Hightailing it away from Layla's car, ready to get this meet and greet over, wondering which bus is the roadies. As I walk around the side of the bus, there he is in all his cocky glory leaning against the bus, one foot behind him propped on the bus cigarette in hand looking deep in thought. He notices me, flicks his cigarette, and walks in my direction a grin playing upon his face.

"Why don't you let me take your bag?" He asks; a little too late to start kissing my ass don't you think, I say to myself.

"No thanks. I'm quite all right carrying it by myself." I politely decline, even though polite is the last thing I want to be to him. As if he didn't hear me, he tries to grab my luggage away from me. "What part didn't you hear, the no thanks or the part where I said I am all right?" I ask, on my last nerves why he is still trying to pull the bag out of my hand; I pull it back as if we are playing tug-o-war with my belongings.

He chimes in "Let me just help you." On top of everything with Layla, he adds in, and my day just keeps getting better.

"Your chivalry is unneeded." As soon as I push the last word out, with as much grace as I can manage, the zipper breaks. At the same time, he finally let's go. Ending with me falling flat on my ass with everything I packed littering the sidewalk surrounding me. I look up at him mortified. His grin is still in place but with a hint of mischievousness, almost as he planned for this to happen. And then I notice we're not alone. What is it about this guy that brings out the worst in me? The entire band is now outside, along with what I surmise to be the roadies. Just staring. At me.

That's when I feel the almost uncontrollable tears threaten to break from the dam and fall. My eyes are glazing over in a clouded mist. Don't let him do this to you. Just breathe, and you'll be fine. You can either let him know he affected you or act as nothing happened. I opt for the latter, using everything inside of me to keep the tears at bay.

Raising myself to my knees, all the while still ignoring Steele, who has made no move to help me, I start collecting my clothes and placing them back into my now broken suitcase.

As I start picking up the last remnants of my personal effects, a pair of muscular thighs join me, meeting his eyes he pulls out his hand and introduces himself.

"Liam," he says.

And that was enough. Enough for me to allow this stranger to help me. When we are done, he grabs my bag carefully holding the door of it shut to his side with one hand and yanks me up by my forearm with the other.

"You're rooming in our bus." He informs me.

Outraged. "Like hell I am, I'm not going anywhere near that asshole!" I yell.

"Calm down Princess. You'll be fine. Trust me. You will be much safer rooming with us." He says in a soft soothing tone.

"Safer? Safer how? Obviously, this man has it out for me. That's why I am here in the first place." I argue. I wonder how he conned Professor Roberts into forcing me to go along with the horrible idea.

"He doesn't have it out for you, and he didn't plan for you to be our intern, hell he didn't plan for us to have any intern. But if you want to fight it fine, I'll let you have a say. You can room with five self-controlled men, your own bed, some semblance of privacy and you can even have a say in the grocery lists or you can room on a bus filled with ten other guys, who are most certainly slobs, and who will try not to let you have any privacy at all. Also, they eat pizza almost every night."

I'm pretty sure he was just trying to sell himself to me, but I could also see the sincerity in his eyes. "I'll accept, under two conditions and I will not budge on it." I refuse to be taken advantage of! If Steele arranged this then he can pay. "I want this to be a paid internship. At least four hundred dollars a week and when we stay at a hotel I want my own room." I would compromise if he put up a fight on the pay. Whatever money I make I'm going to donate, so they might as well donate a small sum.

"Done." Liam says, without hesitation.

"Lead the way..."

He walks me over to the bigger of the two busses. It's about forty-five feet long with their bands name Steele's Army plastered all over it. Liam starts explaining how the first show of the tour is in Boston. Not understanding why we were all here today getting on the bus when their first show was here in Boston. Couldn't they have waited to board the tour bus until tomorrow? I could have prolonged getting on this godforsaken bus with that selfish prick.

Walking onto the bus, he points out where the refrigerator and cupboards are, how there are certain foods I shouldn't eat, that every member of the band has one particular item they get just for themselves. Liam's' being peanut butter Oreos. Past the kitchen area, is the living room. On the left side is the couch it could seat up to six people, and a table on the right. An LCD television is placed on to the wall, kiddie cornered so wherever you are sitting you would have a view. I also notice shelving with gaming stations on it. I guess this is what they do for fun. And a little bit further in are beds, six to be exact.

Apparently, they like to have their things already set up so when the show is done, and the meet and greets are finished they can hop back on the bus take showers and pass out. Then on to the next stop, it's also kind of like pre-gaming for their first show, its part of their tradition he tells me. Before they go on stage every night, they sit down on the couch aligned against the wall and make up their set list. Unlike other artists, they never pre-plan what songs they will be performing that night until right before the show. They always change it, never repeating the same songs. I'm actually impressed; it's almost unheard of. I point out sound check. Why not choose those songs then? Liam said they always do the same warm up songs at sound check.

$\mathcal{T}$hree on each side. Enough to fit one body. A ladder going up to the very top bed. All equipped with a mini curtain you could slide closed. Then the bathroom, he opened the door just enough for me to tell he and I would never fit unless we wanted our bodies to be contoured to one another. Liam walks me through a door straight to the back of the bus and tells me it is the main bedroom. It's more or less used for storage. Storing every-one's clothes or extra food. There's an overturned mattress against the wall, he says that if by chance if anyone had a visitor they could use it.

He shows me to a closet that we all will share, and told me I could hang my clothes in there, as well. Also, a large dresser that he made room for me in so I could hide my unmentionables'.

It's actually pretty nice. Better than I had hoped for. If this is what the bands bus looks like, I couldn't imagine what the roadies' looks like. Liam leaves me to myself in the big back bedroom. I start unpacking, hanging my clothes, putting my bras and panties away in the dresser, then grabbing my zip lock bags and stuffing them in the drawer too. I doubt there is any room in the bathroom for my shampoo let alone my body. When all unpacked I walk back out into the living area, I see Liam sitting at the table with Steele and because he is the only one who has introduced himself, besides the giant asshole who is currently talking to him, I decide I'll ask him what bunk is mine.

Stepping over to Liam, who is in a whispered conversation with Steele. By the look of his brooding face, I'm betting Gage is reprimanding him about our scuffle outside. Interrupting. "Excuse me, I just want to stay out of everyone's way so could you mind telling me what bed is mine?"

Liam turns his head to mine; his lips locked into a smile. Stop staring at his gorgeous lips Natalie, get a hold on yourself. "Sure, you're right below Steele. Steele why don't you show Princess here where her bed is." And here I presumed that Liam was on my side.

I'm really hoping the next two months I won't have to sleep beneath this annoying man. Maybe I can befriend one of the other guys, and they'll swap beds with me.

Steele stands up and just starts walking back to the bunk area. He points to the left, "I'm the top, and you're the middle. Also, hate snoring, so if you snore keep it down or buy some breathe rite strips." Not letting me retort he just walks away.

"Asshole" I mutter.

Climbing up the ladder, I slide into my bed and close the green curtain. I look to my right side, and there is a small window also equipped with a green curtain.

I slide the curtain open and take a look outside. It's facing the sidewalk of the hotel where I can see a few roadies still loading their luggage. I also see Steele. He's talking to one of the other band members I have yet to meet.

He truly is breathtaking. Observing his profile, I can make out his features better in the daylight. He has his dark hair pulled back away from his face held together by a rubber band at the nape of his neck. A firm hard jaw with a days' worth of growth in place. He's wearing a dark blue short sleeve shirt that is showing off his black inked tattoos. His nose is straight. Unusual because from the look in his eyes earlier, I would swear this man was keen on violence. Just from his arguing personality, I would expect that someone would have knocked him a good one and broken his nose in the past.

But nope there it sits upon his handsomely rugged face. Naturally, he feels eyes scrutinizing, and we lock. Eyes knowing; the left corner of his lip pulls up. Damn it. This man's ego it way to big. I bet he assumes I find him irresistibly attractive. That I want him. This I can play. No one has ever tempted me, and I am comfortable it is remaining that way. If a fortune five-hundred CEO cannot bring me to my knees. Then a rock-star has no chance to tempt me.

CHAPTER EIGHT

Steele

*M*inx. She's a damn minx. For Liam to think that he has to sit me down and remind me that she wasn't here for my cruelty. Like I was the one who threw all of her clothing and undergarments all over the sidewalk. I was trying to be a gentleman. Knowing she and I got off to the wrong start, she and I need to reach some kind of middle ground. How do I expect my plan to work if we don't at least somewhat get along? Maybe if she would give me a chance to redeem myself or let me in a little. I could see how guarded she was that night on stage, how she seems to always remain guarded.

As soon as Liam shut the door to the back bedroom, so she could unpack I presume, he marched over to me and demanded my full attention.

"Ryan, this girl, she's not as strong as we thought she was. You're an intense guy. For someone like her, you seem overbearing. She was fighting tears out there; I had all I could do to not comfort her. Knowing it would have only made the situation worse if I did." He whispers.

"Jesus. You act like I ran over the girls fucking dog. It was an accident. Her bag looked heavy, so I offered to help. I have no care what goes on between you and her. But when she wants marriage and babies don't come crawling to me for advice." I need to get away from this conversation. Unwanted feelings of jealousy are running through me right now.

This girl is in my head, and I need to kick her out. Looking for an escape from this conversation, said Minx interrupts wanting to know where her bed is. Then Liam does exactly what I didn't want him to do. Offers me to show her to her bunk. Dick. Are all of my band mates against me all of a sudden? They are all aware of what my intentions are, and now they are playing protective of her. Standing up I walk away knowing that she will follow.

I show her where my bed is first, then hers, I offered her a few suggestions on what I don't like. Crowded is how she makes me feel, with her coconut smelling golden brown hair and the devastation that lurks behind her facade of a smile she puts on. It makes me want to ask questions. To prevent myself from doing so, I leave the bus. A cigarette is just what I need.

I pull my pack of smokes out and light one up. Exhaling a puff of smoke, I watch the roadies walking in and out of the bus loading their things in. One walking around with a checklist in hand making sure everything is accounted for. Gage stands next to me.

"So that babe from the other night, I see she made it after all." He says eyeing my reaction. Testing me. Almost.

"Not going to discuss her or what happened so leave it alone." I say shutting it down right now.

"All right man, I had to ask. Anyways, I glimpsed our tour schedule but I didn't beat it into my brain. After the Fleet Center what's our next stop? My ma wants to fly in for our second show. She wanted to be at our first, but you know how she hates Boston." Glad he lets me off the hook. Generally, I'm not a man of many words, and I never explain myself to anyone.

I can talk music all day, any day. If it wasn't for the guys I would be a classic shut in emotionally, but they know when I have had enough I close the conversation down. Liam is the only one who always tries to break that barrier. "Our next stop is in Upstate, New York. I'll find out the exact city tonight; I would tell her to get a ticket to Albany, wherever we are would be within a few hours' drive." I answered Gage.

Six hours later, both buses are packed, and our concert starts in about four hours. The guys and I decide to get both of the buses over to the Fleet Center, when we arrive we will order dinner to be delivered, pre-game then sound check. It sounds like a pretty easy to-do list. In actuality, it's one of the most tiring jobs. Once we exit that stage all we want is a hot shower, and a comfortable bed. Sometimes, also an easy woman.

Instead, we have to hold out on our wants for a couple of hours and do meet and greets. As popular as we are that isn't something we have to keep doing. Many artists believe it's too risky because of how big their fan base is. Doing a meet and greet when you're that popular can open the possibility to a lot of bad situations; others just won't do it because they feel they're above it. Like they don't owe their fans shit.

Therefore, even being exhausted we all still carry our asses out there every fucking night. We do it for free. If they bought a ticket, pit, lawn or orchestra seating they are all welcome to wait in line and meet us. It's something we won't ever stop doing. I want to meet every god damn fan. We stay there, sitting in a little crowded booth on uncomfortable metal chairs until we meet every last fucking fan.

Way we see it, these fans. These everyday hard working people. They buy our albums. Our merchandise and our tickets. Keeping us on the billboards all because they want to hear more from us. We owe them. If all I am able to do is sit until my ass goes numb and sign autographs until my hand is cramping, then we will all keep doing just that.

I owe my life to my fans, unbeknownst to them. It's undeniable that I could have ended up dead the way that my life was headed. My parents lead prime examples of a life you didn't want to have. I wasn't planned, and they held that against me until the end of their days. Mom drank and smoked crack while pregnant, Dad only joining her in those habits. Even when I entered the world, I still wasn't worth enough to them to quit their addictions.

I was in a foster home until I turned eight. My parents somehow convinced the courts that they had mended their ways. They were reborn again Christians, so they said. At eight, I just wanted somebody to care about me. Truly care what happened to me. To love me, I couldn't have been happier when my current foster mom had told me I would be going home. To have my own family back, I was in childhood bliss. Nothing could go wrong in my eyes.

When I met them for the first time they clutched me in their arms, and I felt as if they were my home. This is what I had been waiting my entire life for. I grabbed my plastic bag full of clothes and hopped in their car. We drove up to the perfect house, better then what I had dreamed of. A one story ranch style house, it was a gray blue with black shutters and a metal fence enclosing the spacious yard. I remember thinking about how I could run around all day and play. I yanked that car door open and ran right into the house. As if I had lived there my whole life.

I should have known something wasn't right with these people. My parents at that moment. My father yoked me up by the neck and asked where my manners were. He made me go back outside and knock on the door. To ask to be allowed entrance. Isn't this my house now too? As an adult looking back, I realize I had no chance with those people.

Kids. They dream, they hope, but never really know the true hurt in the world. At eight, I was blinded by love. By nine, I had felt hatred. Toward my parents, toward anyone who I came into contact with. I was pissed off at the world. My parents hadn't changed a bit. Now I was stuck here.

They moved higher. More hardcore. Heroin, Meth. They just couldn't afford it. They had a grand scheme though, brilliant idea. Play the fucking courts. Get their kid back, and then they could get me to steal, pick pockets of strangers, and steal from stores. Whatever it took to get money for their habits.

Wherever and whoever. It had never mattered to them if those people needed what they had. It didn't matter that there was a chance I would get caught or if, in turn, the person I was robbing was to get violent. And if I ever turned up back at home empty handed, well then, they would make sure that I wouldn't walk for days.

Eventually, I graduated school and then got away from that house and them. Staying at friends' houses a few nights here and there, and playing gigs in between. We were lucky that we had only been playing for about a year when discovered. Since then, my parents have both passed. I'm sure rotting in eternal hell. Overdosing on drugs, who would have thought?

They tried to contact me a few times. Once they even had the balls to leave a voice-mail threatening to let my life story out in exchange for money to keep them quiet. I ignored the meaningless ultimatum. They could make empty threats all they wanted I knew they would never reveal any information out of fear of implicating themselves. That's how selfish they were; only ever looking out for themselves... I don't allow people to peer into my book of life. I would never willingly volunteer information about myself only because I don't want anyone to feel sorry for me. I may have been born into shitty circumstances, and I could have succumbed to the life I had. But I changed my situation.

Liam knows all of it. And the rest of the guys have some knowledge, that's enough to satisfy them and enough for me to still remain unaffected by stares full of pity. The only way I let someone in, is through my songs. Each song I have written is a piece of me, in every line. It's the only place in my life where I allow vulnerability. I am now I'm not the only one out there with hardships, battles to wage, wars to fight. But fuck if it doesn't feel like I am alone in this.

Parked at the back entrance of The Fleet Center, Liam goes around checking with everyone what they want for dinner. Usually we don't have time to order out because we don't end up arriving at the venue until sound check so when we're able to we take advantage of it. One of us not having to cook for a night. Fuck yes. Not asking me what I want, he took his cell out and dials the number for a local Italian eatery. Liam knows I am not a person for change; I always get the same thing.

Showering, a must do before the show. I throw some money at Liam and head to the back bedroom to grab some clothes, most likely what I'll be wearing on stage tonight, as well. As I shove the door open, someone else is yanking it back. I stumble, taken aback not expecting someone to be in there. I forgot. This Brunette beauty is with us for the entire summer.

I'm frozen, not able to speak. She's staring at me with weary eyes; mouth pinched as if she's cautious on what to say or do. Is she trying to make me feel guilty? Not sure if I should even speak to her. I don't want to engage in an argument shortly before we have to be on stage. I never walk away from a discussion involving any kind of anger; it's just not who I am.

Sliding my body sideways to let her walk out, showing her I won't bow into her act. She can act like an innocent shy college girl, but I know better.

She has a razor sharp mouth, and she knows how to use it. Amazed that she can have a vengefully determined look one moment, the next a haunted sad look with a flicker of loneliness. This woman is if nothing but many barriers put into place, layers and layers of emotions I have only ever seen reflected back in the mirror.

Like a temptress, it's doing nothing but calling me out, begging for me to strip every single coat she has wielded around herself. Nothing good can come of this.

I enter the room, after having been standing there stuck in place, thinking of her. After changing, I make my way out to the dining area and see everyone sitting around the table already eating.

"Nice guys. Starting without me. Where's the chicken Parmigiana?" I ask mocking an Italian accent the best I could. They all start laughing. Except for her of course. Gage slides over making room for me and hands my food over. We eat in stony silence. I could break it, but I believe everyone is in this awkward mood because of the fiasco hours earlier. No, one sure what to say. My guys are taking turns sending questionable stares in my direction. Possibly hoping Ill break the ice. Fuck them. They want to play protective daddy then they can break the tension.

My guys have mistaken her for having a weak character. So naturally they must protect her from the likes of me. As if I have some nefarious scheme to scar her. If I were honest with myself, the only reason I wanted her was to prove myself. To prove the band is deserving to be where we are. Show her that our music means something that we have worked our way to be here.

Nights before, when she was reclining in that far away seat, I knew she wanted to be long gone. When we performed on stage, she confirmed it for me. She was unimpressed, unfeeling of all of the emotion that we've poured out of our souls into our songs. The more she ignored and stayed unmoved, the more I wanted; no the more I needed to break her.

I should have known that an impromptu invitation would have gone unwelcome, and automatically put her on defense mode. When she joined me at the microphone, and her lips opened with that first note, I knew I couldn't let her go. I haven't had a voice affect me as much as hers in years. A sweet throaty rasp with a hint of pain and some other emotion that she quickly hid before I could hear or even feel it. How did she become such a desperate need that I have to unfold so fast?

Throwing my empty food container away I ask the guys if they want to go over our pregame before sound check. Our pre gaming consists of each one of use choosing three songs each that we want to play tonight. We write the list down and then that's our set rotation for the night. I tell the Minx she can join us backstage and watch the show from the side if she wants. We're going to have her learn the roadies set up starting with our next show.

I haven't decided yet whom I am comfortable with her shadowing. Since she'll be spending copious amounts of time with the guy, I want it to be someone I can fully trust. She answers with a short "I'll think about it."   Whatever. She won't have a choice tomorrow night. With the set list, completed we get off the bus and head into the arena through the guest only entrance.

Sound check goes easy and fast. We have enough time to go back into the dressing room, have a few shots, and usually I would be chanting over and over again what city we were in so I wouldn't forget. But since we've been here for a week or so it's already ingrained. I use what time I have nursing a glass of tequila. I don't particularly like going on stage shitfaced. It can only lead to bad choices ending with really bad consequences. So I let the guys enjoy their fun and search the minx out.

Walking around the halls backstage, I don't spot her pretty little face anywhere. I ask a few roadies, and they haven't seen her either. Guessing she must have decided to just stay on the bus. Unquestionably aggravated by it, I stop searching and head back to the guys with a few minutes to spare.

"Find what you were looking for?" Gage questions.

"I wasn't looking for anything, or anyone I just wanted to make sure Jack got our set-list." I snap back.

"Sure, that's what you were doing. Are y'all ready to start this fucking tour?" Gage shouts ecstatically.

The guy has an infinite amount of happy energy. I envy it. Zepp places five shot glasses down, fills them to the brim with Jameson's, and hands them out.

"Bottoms Up" he says as he smacks his glass against mine.

Downing mine in one swig, I let the burn set in and breathe it out. Sitting my now empty shot glass down on the dressing room table, guys following suit we walk to the stage.

"Hello Boston! Are. You. Ready. To. Fucking. ROCK."

CHAPTER NINE

Natalie

*O*verhearing Steele ask one of the roadies where I was, I cowered into the wall hoping to make myself disappear from his view. He is way too intense. Every time, our eyes, meet his emotions flow out and push onto me. Holding me captive whenever we are within vicinity of each other. It is best if I stay out of his way, this attraction that I feel only lust, nothing good can come out of.

Ryan Hurst, a mystery I want to investigate and unravel. Denying myself an interaction with the man of the hour, day, week, next two months I run off back to where I had entered only moments before. The crowd. Not a fan of strange hands groping my ass, I usually stay in the back. Yes, even when I am an obsessed fan of the performer.

I need to hide though I do not want Steele spotting me in the audience. The first place he would look is in the way back. So I hide, right in plain sight, in the pit. Promising myself, I won't linger too long. I pull my hood up on my sweatshirt to hide myself from view to blend in. I missed the opening acts. It wasn't as crowded as now. Thinking it was best for me to join when everyone was mashed into one another.

As the lights dim down, one by one the guys take place on the stage. I've spent the better part of today with them, from what I've seen Steele is the leader, and there's no question as to why or how that came to be. The man is demanding and domineering; from my experiences to date he is like that in every aspect of his life.

I see Ryan take hold of the microphone and say his intro, causing everyone in my area to start jumping up and down, some asshole spilling quite a bit of his beer on me before snapping it back upright in his hand. I can't even hear what he's saying because everyone is screaming back, mostly obscenities even including some sexual offers.

I slide out of the spot I was in, not wanting to take a chance on drenching myself in alcohol even further. While pushing through other concert goers, they start their first song, one I haven't heard before. I end up in between a woman who's jumping up and down, and pulling her arm back and forth. Her elbow coming pretty damn close to my face each time. And behind me is a guy, with the body of a defensive linebacker, let's hope he decides not to mosh, it certainly wouldn't end well.

When the woman isn't jumping around like a goddamn kangaroo on crack, I end up with a pretty decent view of the stage. Taking Layla up on her advice, to opening my mind, taking advantage of the opportunity that was forced upon me. I listen; I close my eyes and just take it all in. Allowing Steele's voice to take me to the emotions, the place that he is singing about. His song, it must be his. Singing with such strong conviction, about loneliness, desperation, hate. Such contradiction, I wonder what situation he was writing about in his life to have written this, doubtful that anyone but him wrote this. No one can sing a song with such raging passion if they didn't own it. And owning this song is exactly what he was doing on that stage when I opened my eyes.

Wrong. I was wrong about him. I do not have to be a fan of his music to appreciate his artistry. Writing lyrics is an art, an extremely hard one, you bear your soul, allowing strangers in, allowing them to understand what you have felt at some point in your life. If the song weren't yours, everyone would see past the facade. It won't sound real; a fan cannot connect to something unreal. Disconnecting myself from his words, from his soul weakening voice, I untangle myself form the crown and run back to the tour bus.

Rather than be around when they get back from the meet and greet I decide to hide in my bunk. Steele will know when he sees me that I heard. Once I was told my eyes were an open book, try as I might to lock myself into a box I am forever failing at concealing my emotions. I need time, time away from his demanding prying eyes. Lifting my pillow up, I lift my iPod out from under my pillow and unravel the earphones, hoping I won't even hear them come back before I drift off to sleep. Hitting shuffle, the most poetically beautiful voices start singing, Mumford & Sons.

Ghosts That We Knew, is such an emotional song. One filled with pain and courage. I close my eyelids to just listen and feel the music that's pumping into my ears.

*W*iping tears from my eyes, I hit repeat and let the song play over and over. Until I fall asleep.

Waking up, the earphones must have fallen out; I overhear the guys talking. They must have come in not too long ago. Trying to maintain the appearance that I am still asleep, I overhear them. I recognize Steele's voice, but there's another one. I haven't officially been introduced to him, but I know his voice. It's Zepp.

"I don't fucking care if she's sleeping Zepp, let me the fuck through! She could have gotten herself hurt with that childish act she pulled out there."   Steele screams. Shit.

How could he have seen me? I made sure to blend myself in. Only staying for one song.

"Ryan, go calm yourself down. This is something we can discuss in the morning, help her understand why it isn't safe for her to do something like that. Raging at her like a goddamn bull will not help. Come on man, you remember when we would sit at the fucking bar while our opening acts would perform. We had to go with the changes; she's not used to this." I hear Zepp argue back.

I cringe inwardly. Closing my eyes hoping Zepp doesn't let him go, only for him to confront me.

I hear the door of the tour bus open then shut with a slam. Suddenly my curtain is slid open. It's Zepp a hard glint in his eye. "I've held him off as long as I can. When he comes back in here no one else including me will be able to stop him."

He must have noticed how tight I was clutching the blankets underneath my body, his face softens. "Just stay in here, get some

sleep, and Natalie, and please don't pull a stunt like that again."
With that, he slides my curtain back to close, and I hear his
footstep's retreat and then the bus door shut gently.

Unlocking my IPod I check to see what time it was, eleven
pm, he must have ran right off stage as soon as they closed out
the show. Fortunately, the meet, and greet was now and from
what I've heard they should be gone for quite a few hours. Putting
the earphones back in, and I drift off to sleep.

I run to the door wondering who would be knocking this late
at night. Layla right behind me, I open the door to a police
officer, he asks my name, then Layla's. His name is Officer
Pettys, he tells us to get our shoes on and to join him outside.

"It's an emergency." He states.

Instantly my palms start sweating, and my body starts
shaking, uncomfortable about the unknown. And right now there
is something definitely wrong.

When Layla and I go outside the police car is already pulled
up, officer behind the wheel. We just get in, not asking any
questions. I can tell he doesn't want to speak. Maybe trying to put
off the inevitable, not wanting to irrevocably change our lives. I
know that this is a dream. My body still in a sleep haze. I feel like
I am a third person looking in from the outside. Watching myself,
watching my life about to crumble. Everything I had ever thought
I knew about life was about to change forever.

Body still asleep, my mind still awake, I try to push through
this. It's a dream, a recurring one actually more like a nightmare.
I relive this memory quite often; I have lost count of how many
times I've had this same exact nightmare. Hating that my mind is
stuck in limbo, I can hear people around me awaken. I can smell
food cooking eggs and bacon. All I want is to wake up fully, so I
try to push through the haze of distant memories. Trying to clear
my mind, to fly away from this dream and push that tragic night
back into my subconscious.

Embarrassing myself, I awake with a scream. My curtain is
thrown open, and Steele's face is in mine, checking me over.
Prying into my personal space. I'm speechless. My body is
shaking. From the embarrassment or the churning of my gut, I

haven't decided yet. I shove Steele out of my way and jump off the bunk running to the bathroom. My body smashes into another body, this one hard. It knocks me on my ass.

I don't even glance to see who it was, I pick myself up and scurry to the bathroom. Locking the door, I lift the toilet seat; pull my hair away from my face and vomit. I vomit until there is nothing left, my abdominal muscles cramping because of the heaving, my eyesight sprinkled with white dots from lack of oxygen.

Sweat dripping down my face, I stand up and turn the faucet on to the sink. Cupping water in both of my hands, I splash the water upon my face letting it run down, mixing with my sweat. Looking in the mirror, the stranger I see, the sadness that consumes me, I know she is me. But I do not recognize her, not anymore.

Forcing myself to ignore my reflection I spy someone's toothpaste sitting on the small counter, since mine is currently in a zip-lock bag in the back bedroom I squirt a little onto my finger and rub the toothpaste along my teeth and over my tongue. Spitting out the toothpaste, trying to wash away the acidic taste in my mouth. Someone starts pounding on the door.

"Who is it?" I ask. No answer. Pounding resumes.

"What do you want?" No Answer.

Fuck this, I am the only woman on this damn bus the least they can give me is some semblance of privacy.

Whipping the door open, hand still in a fist, pounding ferociously it stops inches from my face.

"What! What is such an emergency, you could not wait until I was done?" I groan.

He doesn't say a word. He shoves me back, far enough back in this cramped bathroom, so that he can fit in here, as well. Shutting and locking the door, he's looking at me, eyes hard with not a trace of his usual smirk.

Clueless as to what I could have done I start attacking "You have no right coming in here, assuming you had permission. Who do you think you are?" There's nowhere to move. I'm stuck. My back is up against the wall, the shower on my right, toilet on my left. He is near the sink, about a foot away from me, and he's inching closer. I'm stuck, watching his feet and waiting for a reply. I'm doing all I can not to look up.

I don't want to know what he has to say. With the look, he had on his face last it couldn't be anything good. His feet meet mine, and it's as if I have no control over myself, he does this to me. I look up, into his eyes, no longer filled with anger, but lust? Shooting my eyes back down, to the ground, to our feet, where our toes are meeting. It's impossible; there is no fucking way he is looking at me like that right now.

My body reacting; I feel goose bumps sprout all over my skin, my breathing picking up and I can barely disguise it. He angles his body even closer, still not touching I feel his breath on my ear.

"You my Minx, would do well remembering that this is my tour bus, so wherever I choose to be, whenever I want to be, I can."

I shake. Anger replacing the hormonal reaction I was previously having now draining away.

This man must truly believe he is God, the all-fucking-mighty. I'll be damned if I let him think he can walk all over me. Reminding him, I am not another piece on his long list of property he can run. "Oh, Steele." I say, with a flirtatious roll of my eyes, drawing him in. I align my lips with his ear and whisper in "Babe, it really would be best for you to remember, you are the manipulative asshole who forced me to be here. Just because I am here does not mean, in any way shape or form, that I want to be here. That I want you or at any rate I even like you. Just, Leave. Me. Alone."

He stands still. Still processing what I said. I shimmy against his side and leave the bathroom while he will still let me.

Keeping my emotions in tight rein, I put a smile on my face. The facade always holds people back from asking questions, not that anyone ever truly cares. It's a show allowing some to put on an air of generosity and faking sincerity in caring what happens to you. No one gives a shit about the fucked up half-life I have lived for the past five years. Truth be told though, I fair pretty well with that.

It could be the guard I have around my heart that only Layla has ice picked her way into. Entering the back bedroom. I lean into the closed door, allowing myself to have a temporary mental breakdown. Tears begging to be released from my eyes, I permit them. Clutching the door like it's my life raft, keeping me uprooted from falling to the floor in a severe panic attack.

As the shuddering of emotion leaves my body, my tears slowly start forming. I feel pressure against the door. Someone is trying to enter the room. I'm praying it isn't Steele. Not now. He would only stampede over my feelings. He's not caring of anyone else but himself. I wipe my tears on the sleeve of my shirt just hoping that my eyes aren't as puffy and swollen red as they feel.

I recognize the face that slowly enters the door. Almost with a question as to whether he could enter or not. But as soon as he sees my face he grants himself that permission. Slowly closing the door behind himself he turns around to face me, he's gorgeous, and I laugh out loud at the irony of it all meanwhile I probably sound like a damn fool.

What are the chances, here I am still recovering from an emotional overload, crazily laughing and in walks the angel of sin in all his glory. Showing pity and kindness in his hazy green eyes, he holds out his arms to me offering comfort.

Without thinking, I wrap myself up in him. Relishing in the comfort, usually Layla would be that one, to hold me. But for now he will do. Anchoring me down, with his muscular arms, I snuggle my face into his shirt, breathing him in. He smells of cinnamon and warmth. I wrap my arms around him, as far as I can reach and hold him tightly.

We say nothing to one another, an air of understanding interlacing between us, he holds tighter, squeezing me so tight I don't know where I end, and he begins. We stand there for a while, giving each other our strength and holding our own weakness. My head lying on Sin's shoulder, the door, is thrown open, and my eyes interlock with none other than Steele.

CHAPTER TEN

Steele

Twenty minutes earlier.... Laying in my bed, humming a tune that has been stuck in my head for days, I am trying to let the lyrics come to me. Song writing is a pretty long progress. How much do you want to reveal your inner struggles to your fans? Making yourself vulnerable to judgment, to people assuming they know what your song is about. You can write about any battle you have had in your life and just dismiss any ideas about it meaning something more with the swipe of your hand and a wink to a fan or reporter.

Many of the songs that my band has performed and laid down in the studio, I have written, and every word is from experience. But when asked about the meanings behind the songs I always comeback with some smart ass made up lie. Our drummer Jason also inputs songs on the regular. Some we've collaborated on. I can hear every instrument playing in my head, but the lyrics just won't come.

Giving up, I open my curtain and make my way to the ladder located at the end of my bed. I'm three beds high in the air. Even at six-two I am not jumping to the ground. Fuck that. I would rather look like a pansy then possibly break a bone. Shits not fun and it hurts. Grabbing ahold of the steps on the ladder, I hear a shrill scream almost causing me to lose my grip and fall. I realize it's from the Minx's' bunk.

Ripping open her curtain, she's laying there on her bed sweat beading down her face, body shaking. She's breathing. That's my main concern the other being what in the fuck had scared her. Not saying a word she shoves me back and jumps from the bed. Walking through Liam like a blockade in her path. She runs to the bathroom.

I'll give her a few minutes. That is all though. For some reason, her scream cut into my gut. I could feel the pure fear she had felt. Wanting to make sure that she will be all right I proceed to the bathroom. Turning the knob it refuses to budge. The Minx locked it.

Screw this. There is no way she is going to lock me out. She had to have known I would go chasing after her. I start pounding on the door repeatedly. Not giving in until she answers.

She yells to me "Who is it?"

Oh, my Minx, you know who this is; I say to myself.

"What do you want?" she asks a little more angered now.

I'm not answering her. She's playing a game. She knows who it is, and she knows that I want to check on her.

She whips the door open as I am about to knock again for the hundredth time; I catch my fist right before it hits her in the face. I would never be able to forgive myself if I were to have accidently hit her.

"What! What is such an emergency you could not wait until I was done?" She's pissed.

Probably because I witnessed a moment of weakness. A weakness that shows how vulnerable she really is. I push her in farther, so as to allow me to close the door. I don't want everyone overhearing our conversation. I lock the door and turn back to face her. She looks like a deer caught in the headlights. Frozen. Possibly not expecting me to lock the door, I'm not a God damn pervert. Her virtue is safe with me, but she doesn't need to know that just yet.

She goes on the defense. Calling me out. That I don't have permission to just shove my way into the bathroom, and something about not giving her privacy. I just drown her nonsense rambling out.

I stare at her, fully taking her all in. She's a spitfire that's for sure. She won't just take it and sit back down. Testing her limits, I step closer and closer. Seeing how far she will let me go, at what point will she set a boundary. She is fucking gorgeous. Such pert little lips, I would love to glide my tongue over. To taste her. At this second, all I want to do is pull her body to mine, feeling her supple curves grinding against me.

I need to get the fuck out of here, leave right now. Before I make a big mistake, a mistake that the guys or I would never let myself live down. This Minx perceives to be an innocent, untouched by men yet completely broken. It's not a wise or safe choice. But I can't help wanting to rile her emotions, not retaining any control of myself I lean in as close as I can without touching her.

I whisper in her ear, also a sly move so I can smell her hair. "You my Minx, would do well remembering that this is my tour bus, so wherever I choose to be whenever I want to be I can."

Fuck. Even I can hear the lust and implications in my voice. The scent of her hair, fruity coconuts is making my mouth water. If I thought she wouldn't put up a fight I would bury my nose in deep and inhale.

I pull back, risking a glance in her eyes.

I shook her, not enough to crack her. Still. But shook all the same.

"Oh, Steele." she says, flirtatiously.

I hate that she won't say my name. Her tone has caught me off guard, did I go too far?

"Babe, it really would be best for you to remember that you are the manipulative asshole who forced me to be here. Just because I am here does not mean in any way shape or form that I want to be here. Or that I want you or at any rate I even like you. Just leave me alone."

Liar! I want to shout, but she sidesteps me and leaves the bathroom. I relock the door behind her waiting for my hard cock to deflate. What is happening to me where aggressive altercations are turning me on?

I reach in my jeans and readjust my still semi-hard cock. I unlock the door. This conversation isn't over between her and I. Glancing around the bus; I don't see her anywhere. She couldn't

87

have left because we are currently driving to our next show somewhere in upstate New York.

I see Gage lying on his bottom bunk.

"Have you seen Natalie?" I ask.

"Yeah, she's in the back bedroom, with Liam." He tells me.

"What are they fucking doing in there?" I yell, blaming him that they are alone. No one can resist Liam. My number is way higher than his but that's because of his extremely high standards. Most women will never adhere to them. Liam is a picky motherfucker, and I will be damned he decides that Natalie fits his bill.

"I don't fucking know Ryan. Why don't you bust the door down and go find out?" Gage says, teasing me.

"Well I can't just leave her alone in that fucking room with him." I say storming to the back bedroom door. Shoving it open, the scene before me has fire lining each and every vein in my body.

Natalie is cocooned in Liam's arms, both there on their own volition. What feels like betrayal paralyzes me. Why am I feeling this way? She's nothing to me. No one. If she wants to fuck Liam, wants to be a non-self-respecting groupie that's fine by me. Let them have at it. I'm not going to be in the middle of a temporary sex affair because with Liam that is all it will ever be.

I look at her, hatred pouring out of me and I exit the way I came in. Quietly this time.

Just meeting him, and she is already wrapped up in his arms. It's a wonder she even fought going on this tour. Walking into the kitchen area, Gage is making breakfast. The smells of bacon and eggs permeating the air. I sit down at the table waiting for the food to be set out. Pulling out my cellphone, inputting our destination into the internet search to see if there are any attractions for us to revel in. We have two shows at the Time Union Center. Good thing because that means we will be staying in a hotel.

I send a text to Mel asking what hotel we will be staying at not wanting to bother the driver. That way I can plan out a bit of a retreat for the guys and I. Maybe there are some local bars we can hit up. I would do well with a fresh piece of ass. Surely needing to get the Minx out of my head. Thoughts of her are only bound to get me in trouble with one of the guys. Every time I think of her my cock swiftly reacts.

Mel replies just as Gage sits plates full of bacon, eggs, French toast and sausage on the table. We will be rooming at the Hilton in Albany, for three days. Arriving the day before the show and leaving directly after the meet and greet then on to Buffalo, NY. Noticing that everyone has joined the table. I look to Natalie. When she takes, notice that my eyes are on her she downcast hers.

Guiltily. My mind running fucking crazy. I race through all thoughts of what they could have possibly done since I left them alone. Well if she wants to piss me off, seemingly on purpose, two can play that game.

"We will be in Albany tonight, not playing until the day after next. I thought we could go out scoping around for some new pussy." I announce. All the while staring at her.

She flinches, as if I cut her, somewhere inside. Deep inside. Hiding it as soon as she saw that I took notice. Ignoring her, pretending ignorance of her feelings, I glance around the table. Liam's mouth is wound tight, annoyed maybe, a little pissed. Zepp, Gage and Jason agree readily all nodding their heads secretly. I look to Liam, in question if he's joining or not.

"I think I'll pass tonight. I'm not feeling well anyways."

Floored, I know he's lying. I would hate to admit it but because of him jealousy and I are becoming fast friends. That the Minx would even want to be in my presence when she clearly detests mine, while he and I are best fucking friends, is beyond my comprehension.

Thus making me want to ruin whatever connection they have between them. "Yeah, you don't look so well Liam." Turning my glare to Natalie "I don't think it's your scene but you could join us if you wanted."

And with that I rise from the table, dismissing the conversation. Going to the back bedroom, grabbing my clothes. In need of a shower. For years, nothing has come close to flaring my temper. Unbelievable that this Minx, within days of meeting me, is like putting a match to gasoline.

*S*teaming hot water, pouring over my body. I close my eyes and picture Natalie, how I previously saw her in the bathroom earlier today. With lust filled eyes. Imagining her opening her swiping her tongue over her lips. Teasing me, begging for my cock to enter her mouth. I slowly glide my hand down to my rising cock. Wrapping my hand tightly around my growing length. The water acting as a lubricant I start to slowly stroke it. Picturing her on her knees, mouthwatering, pleading for me to fuck her face. Not able to deny her, needing her mouth, as well.

I slam my cock in her mouth, again and again. Only allowing her short gasps of air. Furiously stroking my cock, that is now beyond rigid, as hard as I have ever been. So close, so, so close. Yanking my cock out of her mouth, I demand her to stand up and bend over, succumbing to her need, greedily she complies.

I lift her skirt, push her panties aside then grip her hips and slam my entire cock into her dripping wet pussy. I can feel her vaginal muscles contracting around my cock, on the cliff of orgasmic bliss, myself on the verge of combusting inside her pussy, I reach around and start rubbing her clit franticly.

Opening my eyes as my dick starts pulsating, spilling my seed all over my hand. Dramatically disappointed, shameful to admit it's the best sex I have had in a long time that I can remember. Mind made up – I must fuck the Minx out of my thoughts. There is no way she could ever live up to that one fantasy, even if given many a night to make it possible.

Drying my body off, someone starts pounding on the door. A new habit quickly catching on around here. Wrapping the towel around my hips, I whip the door open. Of course, the object of my fantasy in the flesh.

"See anything you like?" I say catching her off guard. Closing her then opened mouth

"Please, I have seen much better." She rushes out, trying to convince herself or me I am not sure.

"Then how can I be of help?" I ask.

Trying to hold my hands by my side, the overwhelming need to yank her into the bathroom with me and fuck her up against the wall is almost will-breaking.

CHAPTER ELEVEN

Natalie

Steele escapes the table before I can tell him I am unwilling to accept his invitation to join the band in a night out participating in drinking and pussy scoping. He has to be the most frustrating person I have ever had to share oxygen with only inviting me out of obligation to the band.

I could feel the thick fog of tension when he made it bluntly clear the sole purpose of visiting an alcohol establishment was to get laid. Under the table, Liam had grabbed my hand and gave me a reassuring squeeze. Choosing not to go, to be an unwanted guest. If I had chosen to go, I could easily predict that I would be left behind when they all found what they were looking for.

Definitely not my scene. And Ryan Fucking Steele knew it. His asinine arrogant attitude was way too much for me to handle right now. Overbearing ogre. I should go just to mess with his head. Show him that I can become a chameleon, blending into whatever atmosphere I am surrounded by. Parading around like I belonged.

I'm feeling the need to confront him. To turn his views on a backwards axis. Forgetting Liam's hand was still on mine, I let go and rush to the bathroom where I saw he retreated minutes earlier.

Knocking on the door loudly, impatient to tell him that his challenge, as I view it was accepted. Steele pulls the door open rapidly, almost stumbling I catch myself. He's naked, towel around his waist but naked nonetheless.

Think, Nat, think. His being naked inches away from me has my bodies hormones running rampant. My mouth hanging open surely my salvia is about to start slowly dripping out of my mouth. Unaware of the sexual need firing in my veins, he half smiles a snarky grin.

"See anything you like?" Cocky bastard.

"Please, I have seen much better." I most certainly lie. The man is sex in a bottle. A drink if picked up, I would never be able to put down. An addicting bad habit.

"Then how can I be of help?" He asks. If you only knew. An assuming asshole, he doesn't see my innocence, at this moment he is the closest I have been to seeing a man naked. Ever.

Looking away from him in all his glory, I can feel my face flushing, my heart pounding in my chest and my stomach is swirling with butterflies. These feelings of attraction I have never felt. Only with him. Why couldn't it be with someone else, anyone else? I start counting the tiles, trying to calm my body. These unwanted reactions to him.

"Are you there Minx?" He says in a light husky tone.

No longer able to ignore him, I look up. Eyes smoldering. He isn't as indifferent as he proclaims to be. Before I can answer him, he grabs on to my hand hard and pulls me then spins me around. My back slams the door shut.

My arms pinned above my head, held down by one of his hands.

I cannot hide from him how badly he is affecting me; my legs are shaking, adrenaline firing throughout my system. My lungs are gasping for air. I don't know what I am more scared of, him or embarrassing myself. Like my natural shell protecting myself, I go into automatic defense mode.

"Have you finally lost it Steele?" I say taunting him.

He grins. Keeping one hand over mine, he reaches forward with his free hand and cups my chin. Forcefully yanking my jaw up, so I have to look him in the eyes.

"No Minx, I think I have finally gained it."

He runs his fingertips down my jawline, lightly brushing my neck leaving goose bumps in his touches wake. His fingers stop as they reach the seam of my shirt.

I want to beg him to just do it. Rip my shirt down and touch me. Touch all of me. Instead, he runs his fingers back through the trail he previously paved over my neck then grips the back of my head with his large hand.

Slowly pulling me closer, wanting me to meet halfway. He leans his head in. So close that I can feel his breath on my lips. Unconsciously I run my tongue over my lips. Wetting them, anticipating his tongue gliding over my lips themselves. Barely an inch apart from our lip's meeting, he pauses. Maintaining distance. My heart is thudding in my chest repeatedly, and I know that he is not unaffected either. I can feel his hard cock rubbing against my leg. Wishing I wasn't still pinned to the door. My vocal chords freeze, unable to say the words that I want to say. Asking him, begging him to just fucking kiss me.

Reminding myself, I am not his first. Nor will I be his last. All I am is a notch, a conquest of sorts on one of his many long lists I am sure.

I mask my emotions, letting the facade of being untouched fall over my face. This angers him. I see the glint in his eyes; he is considering throwing my actions in my face. And that's when I know he has made his mind up. He wants to prove to himself that he could affect me.   He kisses me. Hard. Rough. Demanding. Letting go of my hands, I run one through his hair. The other grasps his neck, pulling him as close as I can. His other hand now free, he pulls me up wrapping my legs around him. I open my mouth up to him, almost too easily. I am greedy for his taste, for his touch.

Our tongues are melding. Lashing. Taking and giving relentlessly. Neither of us submitting to one another. Neither of us feeling completely satisfied, unable to get close enough. We struggle against this battle. I use his hair, pulling him harder against me. He uses my ass, pushing my pussy against his hard cock as close as he can without removing my clothes.

This kiss, our kiss, is the kind of kiss you drown yourself in, refusing the very thing you need to breathe. Oxygen. Because at this moment he is my air.

So caught up in kissing him, I didn't notice that his towel fell to the floor, pooling around his feet. Looking back it probably happened when he picked me up, the slow grinding most likely caused the slow loosening of his towel. For that matter, I don't think he noticed either, both realizing when my hand brushed IT.

He and I stopped kissing instantly, both looking down. It was fucking huge. I had never seen a penis, but I am sure this wasn't a normal one. It couldn't be. If it were I think there would many, many women walking around legs bowed.

I wanted to explore it, examine it, to learn what made it hard, what made it get off? What made Steele get off? Reaching out my hand, this time to purposely touch it. Aiming to rub the head of his penis, where there was creamy liquid already forming. Then a hand, Ryan's hand, smacked mine away.

Looking up, he was staring at me. A disgusted look on his face directed at me. He looked like he was going to be sick; my touch had made him ill. Tears of utter humiliation wanted to break free, not wanting him to see and embarrassed I ran out of the bathroom to my bunk.

Laying down in my bed, closing the curtain. Trying to forget what just happened between Ryan and me.

I roll over to face the miniature window I stare out onto the Thruway. It's in the middle of the afternoon, surprisingly we seem to be the only ones driving on this stretch of I-97. We are headed north to upstate NY. My view is tree after tree. Sometimes there is a break in between that's filled with rock walls. Seeing warning signs for deer crossings and falling rocks. Home Sweet Home.

Layla is the only one, besides her parents who knows where home for me originally is. Not even school, they believe I am from Boston; I transferred a few months before senior year in high school. I didn't want to have to explain to anyone where home truly was, or why I would have wanted to leave.

When you meet someone in college, the first questions usually are,

"What is your name?"

"Where are you from?"

"What's your major?"

I never want to answer any of those questions; it's no one's business. I would rather stay to myself and keep my life private. Glad we are going so far north way past my hometown, it's a town where everyone would rather stay their entire lives then break free and explore what the world has to offer. My parents were from Beverly Hills; that's where they were raised in luxury and with lots and lots of money. They thought it would be better to raise their only child in the backwoods.

Of course, we had a glorious mansion, nothing but the best. But it was country, all trees and rolling hills. Not too far away from the city that you couldn't take a day trip. I will never go back there willingly; I sold the mansion. Moved in with Layla's family which wasn't that much easier seeing as how my pervious childhood home was across the street. I promised myself once I made it out I wouldn't return. Layla has always understood this; she was the only person I had ever shared my plans for the future with. Her parents, my guardians at the time never showed any interest. I think my leaving made it a little easier on them, seeing me every single day only served as a reminder of the tragedy that had happened.

*M*y mind going back to that lingering feeling of anger still reeling in my body. The frustration of earlier quickly dissipated any last effects of sexual attraction that I had been feeling. What in the fuck was Steele trying to pull back there? He is hot one second then cold the next. Cold mostly, almost heartless. I need to take away his power over me, cutting off all emotional access. Avoid him at all costs. Never allowing him the opportunity to be alone with me.

Liam will help me, once I tell him my plan and reasoning's. The sense of comfort with Liam is foreign. I have only felt this way with Layla, but she has been there since the beginning.

My emotions running rampant for the past few days has been extremely exhausting. Sleep wanted to claim me, and I was if not anything but a willing victim. Grabbing my iPod out from underneath my pillow, I plug my earphones in and insert them in my ears.

Clicking my music stored on my phone, knowing that listening to music is the only way I have the possibility of not having a nightmare. I hit shuffle all songs and one of my many favorites by Bon Iver starts playing...

"Skinny Lover," is a soul soothing melody of strings on a guitar played alongside Bon's emotional inducing voice. If there were one thing that would help me forget what I'm feeling right now, it would be this.

CHAPTER TWELVE

Steele

*W*hat did I just let fucking happen? God damn it.

Jerking myself off and releasing in the shower did nothing to whet my appetite for her. When I opened the door and saw her realizing I was in nothing but a towel, her face flushing, I couldn't help myself. I needed to feel her, taste her, and I needed her to submit to me. She didn't. Not once. It was a battle of wills. Who would break first?

She had tasted of spearmint. I couldn't get enough. I wanted to strip her of her clothing and fuck her until she came all over my cock. Now left in the same situation I was when I entered the shower, hard and in need of a fuck. There is no way I am staying on the bus tonight. As soon as we hit the hotel up I am going out, a few shots of liquor and getting laid. I have to get this fucking girl out of my head.

Getting dressed, hating that my cock is still hard, I shove it in my jeans. Needing to express my thoughts, I grab my tattered notebook that I have had for years from my bunk. Sitting down at the now clean kitchen table, I begin to write a song. Still unsure if I want to share it with the band. It would truly showcase how cruel I can be. The words pour out of me...

"You say you want me

That you need me

Then get on your fucking knees and let me see

I say I hate you

That I don't need you

So stand up and run the fuck away

You say you miss me

That you love me

Then get on your fucking knees and let me see

I say I resent you

That I am disgusted by you

So stand up and run the fuck away

You say you crave me

That you liberate me

Then get on your fucking knees and let me see

I say I distrust you

That I can't need you

So stand up and run the fuck away

Why did you listen to me?"

I write many songs, whenever I am inspired by feeling. I am just particular about what songs I share with the world. Not sure if I could share this part of myself. If I could lift that shade to showcase my vulnerability. I close my notebook, saving this song for another day. If I were to get my guitar out right now and start playing while singing these words, they would know what or whom it is about.

I cannot let the guys see she has affected me. If by hate or sexual need. I am not open for any other emotions. I started out wanting to break her, to teach her that every artist puts their blood sweat and feeling into their songs, their art, and their work. Here I am days later, not only wanting to break her music shield but wanting to just break her. Utterly and completely, irrevocably.

Refusing myself that sadistic pleasure for now, I join the guys in the makeshift living room playing video games. Watching them fight one another in Mortal Kombat, I bring up the topic of Natalie training with Rick, our sound engineer, while we are on tour. I, myself, do not feel comfortable leaving her alone with Rick. The guy is a musical genius, he can tune any instrument, hear any differential sounds and pitch and act in a jiff on it.

When it comes to women though, he is always picking up our left over groupies and having them join the roadie bus. Leaving us to face these one night stand women on the regular.

Immediately thinking of him, I feel possessive. He is not going to get his hands on her if I have any say in this. Not wanting to show the guys how much this truly irks me. "So, the Times Union center will be Natalie's first hands on experience. I thought one of us could introduce Rick to her tonight. He can catch her up and fill her in on our shows and shit."

I say, hiding my distaste for Rick.

"Maybe I could teach her a few things, leaving her with Rick only for the actual show." Liam suggests.

Rage and jealousy instantly swirling around in my head, making my blood boil. Of course he would want to spend time with her, unbelievable that I had almost forgotten how chummy they were getting.

"Yeah, sure. Great fucking idea Liam."

I snap out while walking away. Hoping by ending this conversation these feelings will diminish. Refraining from taking my anger out on Liam, my closest friend, my brother. Natalie is working a game, and I am going to figure out what her payout is. I invited her on this god damn tour. Well more like manipulated and paid off her professor to get her on this fucking bus. Either way I could teach her what true music is or what it takes to become successful.

CHAPTER THIRTEEN

Natalie

$\mathcal{W}$aking up, my iPod still blaring music into my ears; I slide the curtain open observing what everyone is doing. From my point of view, I can see the kitchen table where Liam is currently sitting, eating a sandwich. He is a gorgeous specimen of the male race. Rough around the edges but with a smooth, soft soul. Just being near him soothes me, my emotions.

I should inform him of the confrontation between Steele and me. Maybe he can find a way for me not to be alone with him. Or maybe a way I can discourage Steele from wanting anything like that to happen again. I know Steele is a man of non-repetitive bed partners. If and whenever I choose to give myself to someone, it will be with one who wants to share my bed for the long run.

With the state of my life, my past, my present, I can't see where my future is going and if I will ever allow anyone in besides Layla. My gut is telling me that Liam is a decent candidate to share some piece of myself with. Usually my mind overrides my gut instincts but I need someone on this bus who will have my back. Protect me from myself. I am weak, never having anyone from the opposite sex showing any kind of sexual interest in me. I really thought I was stronger than this, until I met Ryan.

The way he made my body catch fire earlier, losing all of my control. Embarrassing myself because I couldn't stop what we were doing. Just coming down from the sexual high when he smacked my hand away. His disgustful stare, instantly cooling the hot quivering need. Determined to keep my innocence, and pride intact. I slide my ass down my bed latching on to the ladder and hop to the floor.

Approaching Liam, he looks up and gives me a small friendly smile. Not asking I squeeze in next to him and start eating the chips off of his plate. He says nothing. We sit there eating in silence. Contemplating how I should bring the subject up, I glance at him nervously and he notices.

"Something on your mind Princess?" He asks, reaching his arm around me and pulling my body up against his side.

Being embraced by him, it feels natural. Almost brotherly. If I ever had one, I am sure this is how it would feel. When we were in the back bedroom, we didn't even speak. Words weren't needed to express how we were feeling; I didn't know his issues nor he mine. Unjudged comfort is what we gave each other. There were no questions that needed asking, and I know whether I shared this with him or not when and if a time came I needed him as a defensive shield, he would take the chance.

Liam is also Steele's friend. His bandmate. I couldn't nor would I ever, want to get in between their friendship. The only way I can see protecting what they have is by discussing it. Letting him know what is racing throughout my mind.

"Can we go in the back bedroom to talk? I would feel better if no one overheard us." I whisper. He doesn't speak. He just slides down the wrap around L- shaped seat pulling my body along with his.

Still holding my hand he leads me to the back bedroom, opening the door shoving me inside and then shutting the door. Grabbing my hand again, he pulls me towards the bed that's up against the wall. He pulls it away from the wall and lets it drop to the floor. Liam sits down and pulls me down with him. Our knees touching, our arms rubbing each other's side by side. He's allowing me time to decide how I want to start this conversation, and for that I am grateful.

I look at him from under my eyelashes. How he the one? Who makes me is feel so comfortable? To most he would be intimidating, hard, gruff, and full of angst. Downright scary. At least six-five with a body builder physique. Short brown hair buzzed close to his scalp. I can see tattoos peeking out of his shirt. This is what people see when looking at him on the outside.

Inside I see a desperate weeping soul, needing to be held and loved. In him, I see myself looking back at me. He's lost. Tears threatening to fall, because his pain is what I feel every day, he pulls me closer. Wrapping me into his arms clutching me close, for the second time that day.

Seems everything is happening in seconds today. At the same time Liam and I fall into an embrace; Steele opens the door. A new first though, Steele doesn't walk away. I wish he had. But he didn't. This time, he rips Liam away from me. Liam lets go willingly. I believe he was trying to deflect a confrontation with Steele. When Liam is about a foot away from me, Steele punches him hard in the face. I don't even bother checking if Liam is ok before I begin lashing into Steele with my words.

"What the fuck is wrong with you?" I scream beyond enraged.

"Nothing is wrong, nothing at all Natalie." He says eerily calm.

This does not satisfy me as a response. You don't just punch your best friend for no reason. I look back at Liam, who is clutching his face and biting his lip. He wants to attack Steele back, but he's also trying very hard not to make the fight worse.

"There has to be something wrong for you to walk in here and punch your best friend in the face." I state. Calling him out.

"How about you answer me a question? What were you two doing in here? What did I interrupt? Is that why you are mad Natalie? Two different band mates in one day. Wow! You're another regular groupie aren't you?" He says, laughing.

Unable to help myself I smack him, open handed on the face, angered beyond belief. I don't wait for an explanation, an excuse or a retort, I storm out of the room.

CHAPTER FOURTEEN

Steele

*S*he fucking smacked me. The amount of things I have ever done with a woman, in all of my experiences, I have never had one smack me. She left me speechless for the second fucking time today. Stuck staring at Liam; he wouldn't even look at me. I can't tell him the truth. Sorry man. When I initially walked in here, I believed you two to be doing something. Turns out you weren't, but I had already reacted and punched you.

Yup. Not admitting that. Even though they weren't doing anything, he shouldn't have had his arms wrapped around her yet again. I trust him with my life. For some reason, I don't trust him with her. Not with my Minx. When in the fuck when did she become mine, my fucking Minx? Tonight cannot get here fast enough.

Ignoring Liam, not wanting to have this conversation with him right now. I will, later when we are off the bus, preferably drunk and searching for pussy. Alcohol inhibiting my mind will make it less likely that our conversation will end in a fist fight. I walk out of the room, taking the same path Natalie took only seconds before.

I make a beeline straight for the driver, asking how much longer it will be until we hit our destination. The Hilton in Albany. He tells me we have about two hours depending on traffic. It's rush hour now, so everyone is on each other's asses bumper to bumper.

Disregarding everyone, I grab some clothes and plan on having yet another shower in one day. With Liam and Natalie shacking up in the back bedroom, the bathroom is the only place I can go to escape. By the time the cold shower cools the uncontrollable burning thrum of my body, we should be at the hotel. Hiding out here in the bathroom is a much better choice. Rather than having to face Natalie and Liam's angry and questionable stares.

Liam seems to have taken to my Minx rather quickly; I'm shocked though because he has known what my plan was all along. She is by no means of any consequence. She's only here temporarily; I desperately want to figure out what it is that's going on between them, but it's none of my business.

Not my place.

I shouldn't care but for some reason the idea of them going to each other for comfort just bugs me. Embracing, holding on to one another like life support, the idea consumes me, putting me in a rage of jealousy.

I need to remind myself why I steer clear of women for the long term. They only want what my life can give them. The money, fame and connections. No one is interested in me. My soul or my pure intentions. All women are fake, materialistic, greedy, and selfish. I don't have room for bullshit like that in my life. Unless she's game for one night, I do not have room for her in my bed.

Stepping out of the ice cold shower, my mind is wagering back and forth on what to do. Should I stay out of her way?

Ignore her? Push her into Liam's arms?

Could I consciously deal with that?

Fuck it. Tonight I'll fuck her all away with a stranger. Fuck away the lingering remnants of her body against mine. Fuck away the hauntingly abandoned looks she's always shoving onto me.

CHAPTER FIFTEEN

Steele

*H*ightailing it off of the bus to light a cigarette that I have been craving for hours. Since we left Boston. The altercation earlier, only making me crave nicotine even more. For the past hour, I have been pacing the bus like a god damn junkie in need of my next fix. Already having an overnight bag packed in hand and not waiting for anyone else, I rush into the hotel lobby.

Ready to take my room key and disappear, I race to the concierge desk. We only use hotels that have employees who respect our secrecy about where we are staying. God forbid someone let that information out. The press would have a field day and so wouldn't every married and unmarried woman above the age of eighteen. It would cause a nightmare of numerous events.

Knowing that Mel used my alias to reserve my room, it's a long standing joke. "Eddie Hurst," I tell the lady at the desk, waiting to check me in. When signing our first recording contract Mel had asked me who my idol was. What musical artist I wanted to live up to. Possibly lifting the bar they had set. I told him Eddie Van Halen. He had laughed at me then, and even laughed when signing us. He thought that it was impossible.

Once we proved him wrong and showed him that we would reach every one of those goals he started calling me Eddie. She pulls up my alias, has me sign a paper about damaging the room and hands me a card. Not caring to look back I stroll out of the lobby to the elevators. Not looking at my key card until the doors of the elevator closed in. Third floor room I think to myself. Hoping luck is on my side that Liam nor Natalie are roomed near me.

On second thought that could be a good thing. Me coming back with a statuesque blonde haired groupie and Natalie seeing.

It has the potential to right things between us. Warn her off before she gets caught up in my shit storm.

Remembering the wager made between us guys, trying to make some kind of amend with Liam, I take my cellphone out of my pocket and send a group text to the guys.

Me: I still have the lead. Anyone game to change that tonight? Bar. Alcohol. Women.

Zepp: Game. What time?

Gage: You're going down dick

Me: Don't want to go out too early, 11?

Liam: I wasn't going to go but sure. You're buying though Steele. You fucking owe me douchebag

Jason: You can't win every time fucker

Me: 11 it is, bring your best bitches

Me: L, it's always on me lol

Putting my cellphone on charge, relief consumes me. Unsure if my actions earlier fucked Liam's and I friendship. I'm close with every one of the guys; they are the only ones I've let know even a bit of myself, my past. What makes me, me. Their friendship and this band are something I do not want to risk, for anything or anyone.

CHAPTER SIXTEEN

Natalie

$\mathcal{W}$atching Steele run off of the bus, afraid to confront his demons head on, Liam grabs the hand that's holding my clothes for the night. He then pulls my overnight bag out of the other, pulling my now empty hand with him and closing his fingers around mine, yanking me of the bus. Zepp, Gage and Jason following behind us. We enter the breathtaking lobby showcasing all of the glitz and glamour of being able to stay within luxury. Black marble tiled floors, varnished wood desk, oversized sofas. And a giant hanging chandelier that looked like it was worth a million dollars.

Also, a beautiful little sitting area consisting of a small library and oversized maroon sofas surrounding a red brick fireplace. Reaching the check-in desk the concierge gave me a quick once over and shuddered in disgust. Seemingly telling me without words that I didn't belong here. That I didn't belong here with these men with devil induced good looks. Luckily for me, even with all of my fucked up half ass life issues, I might be lost within myself and my own mental ass bullshit but I knew that I was worth more. I was worth being judged by my character, not by the people who surrounded me.

I make myself.

I'll be damned if someone was going to belittle or begrudge me into being someone I wasn't. All qualities, my parents, raised me with that I intended to carry on within me. Not giving the lady a chance to get a word out, letting go of Liam's hand. I approached the desk with a big smile laid on my face preparing to smother her with my kindness.

"Hello" quickly looking at her name tag "Joyce" I say in my brightest most over-the-top friendliest voice.

"We all have rooms reserved here, my names Natalie Wright, and this is Li…"

Liam cuts me off "Names Sam Adams."

I look at him, confused. What the hell?

Incredulous, I ignore the obvious lie he just told. Even if he was using a different name, how does he or the other guys not think they would be recognized? They are famous for fucks sake. Years of touring and they still haven't figured this out. Their tours bus, showcasing their bands name, pulled up to the front of the hotel, and they all stepped off not disguised.

It would have been easier if they just told everyone where they were staying. Maybe put it on the ticket stubs the fans attending their concerts bought. Surely everyone in this town knows that a billboard chart topping band is in town putting on not one but two shows in this area. The first being tomorrow night. Shaking my head as I sign the paper Joyce handed me and collect my room key. Liam already has his. Pulling me along to the elevator, he asks what room I am in. Checking my key card.

"Third Floor room 315, you?" I ask curious if we are neighbors for the next couple of nights.

"Same floor, room 314." He says smiling.

Reaching my door, he leans in and places his lips upon my cheek while still holding my hand. A connection I really didn't want to break.

"If you need anything Princess, I'm right next door. Before I forget, hand me your cell." He says, face still close to mine.

"Why would you want my phone?" I ask with uncertainty.

"So I can add my number to your contacts. I changed my mind I am going out tonight with the guys. I just want to fix whatever happened between Ryan and I earlier. If you end up needing to reach me for anything at any time now you can."

He must have changed his mind from earlier this morning when we discussed it at breakfast.

"Oh, Okay." I reply. Bummed.

I let go of his hand, reach in my pocket and grab my iPhone and hold it out to him. When he grabs my phone, I back away upset. Upset that Liam is going out. Leaving me alone, him being the only one I am comfortable with.   Saddened because I feel that he is the only one sincere with his caring and comforting of me besides Layla.

*U*pset that Steele is going out most likely to find a groupie who can't keep her hands off of him. One that will give it up freely. Even after what passed between us earlier. I really need to shake off how much he has gotten under my skin, this man is not good for me.   If I can manage to survive living my life every single day after everything that has happened then I can do this.

Heartbreaker is written all over him. If after earlier he can go out tonight and touch some other woman, kiss another woman, have sex with another woman, then clearly earlier meant nothing to him. Which would mean punching Liam in the face was uncalled for, without reason.

By no means am I a fixer-upper person. I am torn and shattered myself. If I can't fix what I have going on I could never take on the task of fixing or changing someone else. But for once in my life, I want to take a chance, a risk, even if there isn't a jackpot. I have no expectations of him. It seems that most of the time I hate the egotistical man.

Assuming he could touch me, make me feel this way. Overcome with panic, I shrug Liam off and tell him I'm tired and escape to my room. I didn't sign up for this shit. To go on a tour with a band I am not even a fan of. To meet five unbelievably gorgeous men, one who doesn't mind touching me or fighting for me. Then for that same one to leave me alone. Feeling excluded and stuck on the outside.

Slamming the door closed behind me, I start shaking. Tossing my bag on the floor, I sit at the end of the bed and place my head between my knees. One week. One week since my last attack. Hours from the comfort of my bedroom, my home. Hours from Layla. New prospects surrounding me. I focus on my parents and all of the good memories. Waking up every morning before school to share a sit-down breakfast with my parents.

We would talk about our days. What was going on in each of our lives? We were as close as we could be, but they always had obligations to their work and the community. So we made it a point to make sure we still kept our family only time uninhibited.

I'm terrified. Scared as hell. These feelings that have been festering all week are unknown, new to me, and I have no idea what to do with them. Trying to rein it all in all the time, is near impossible. The only chance I have concealing what is waging inside of me is by being near Liam. Unwanted flashbacks of my parent's funeral skipping in and out. I try to shove that memory far back, but it forces itself upon me.

Looking back at my parents' funeral. It was classic. The normal flowers surrounding their caskets and a blown up picture framed of them at the helm. Almost everyone who attended barely knew them. If they did, they had very little to do with us. Hell most I had never met, yet they all felt they could approach me. Giving me the same inconsequential load of bullshit, one after another. Every person stepping up, giving me the fakest most insincere advice.

"They will always be with you."

"I am sure they are looking down on you."

"I am sorry for your loss."

Blah. Blah. Blah. With each and every comment, I fantasized about grabbing their hair, pulling it out. Punching them right in the face. If only for them to stop speaking for a moment.

My parents are dead. No longer here.

I will never see them again.

I will never have another meal with them, celebrate another birthday or ever hear their voices again. There is nothing that I nor anyone else can do to change things. God knows if there were, and it would have been done five years, three months, one week and four days ago.

Experiencing loss is the loneliest thing in the world that anyone at any unexpected time could ever go through.

Sure, many have had to deal with it, paddle their boat across the river of grievance. But not everyone processes the stages of grief at the same pace, or in the same exact order. Not everyone feels death so severely with the loss eating at their souls. To where five years later, it's still controlling every ounce of my emotions', my life, my being.

My soul.

Death- the only thing that can ever be guaranteed out of life. Devastating for survivors, the ones left behind. I can either fall down that never ending drain of despair hiding out forever, or pick myself up one piece at a time and put myself back together. I will forever have the scars and every day is still an incredible battle. At times, I will find myself smiling, a real smile, and it hits me- the guilt. The guilt that I can be happy without them here. That I could laugh without them. So yes when I wake up every morning and feel that rush of pain anew, it's hard to make the decision to get out of bed.

I sludge out of my memories; anger resurfaced at all of the people who pretended to be there then that weren't now.

It was a long hard road to coming to the conclusion that I had few honest people there for me. The ones who had promised, only promised to be there for me because they had a self-interest. Money makes the world go round. How friends are bought hell how family is bought. Not with me. When I saw for myself, I tossed every one of them out of my life.

Self-Preservation. It's what I have done up until now. Until last week, until today.

Repeatedly reminding myself, everyone is only out there for their own gain. Fortunate that my panic attack didn't cause me to vomit. I continue breathing in and out, letting my thoughts settle. I think about what enjoyment I could find tonight. Grabbing my phone out of my pocket, I send a text off to Layla. She replies instantly.

Me: Hey Lal we're in Albany the band has a show tomorrow night. I'm close to freaking out, so close to home. If someone that knew me were to show up. Just... I'm confused.

Layla: About time you reached out to me Nat. Making me fucking worried over here. I knew you would be busy, but I thought I would hear from you before now.

Layla: You'll be behind the scenes. Don't be nervous. You've got this babe.

Me: You're probably right; it's just being here. Our first night in a hotel. Nothing to do.

Layla: Throw a hoodie on and go exploring. Take advantage of this trip babe, you know I would ;)

Me: Sure, maybe. I'll find something.

Me: I'm going to take a shower. I'll text yah later ok. Love ya.

Layla: Love ya too Nat!! Missing you already

Promising to reach her later I decide to take a shower. Grabbing my satchel of clothes, I bring it into the bathroom with me. Sitting it on the counter and starting the shower. While the waters heating up, I look at myself in the mirror. Still unrecognizable. Shady black bags under my eyes that are bright red and puffy. My mouth lightly chapped from the constant licking of my lips from my erratic nerves. I throw my clothes off in a rush to get under that hot steaming waterfall.

Once under the water, I run my hands through the long and thick mass of hair on my head. I once heard this great piece of meditational, stress free advice. When in the shower, I inhale through my nose and slightly exhale through my mouth. There is something so peaceful about it. When I feel like I am carrying the weight of the world, I jump in a hot shower and just breathe. I always end up feeling hundreds of pounds lighter, and my mood lifted.

CHAPTER SEVENTEEN

Steele

After taking quite a few tequila shots in my hotel room from the ungodly expensive hotel mini-bar. Not caring about the cost, I just needed these drinks. I make my way to the elevator. Headed to the concierge desk to ask about all the party hot spots. Stumbling into someone, looking up eyes fuzzy I make out that it's Liam. I clap my hand on his shoulder to balance myself.

"You smell like a God damn brewery, Ryan." He says clearly irritated.

"Pre-gaming my man, pre-gaming."

Walking into the elevator using Liam as leverage to keep my body upright.

"Self-Medicating" he mumbles.

"What the fuck does that mean?" I ask, not understanding what he is implying.

He shakes his head, conversation over before it started. I give in, putting my white flag up before shit gets deep and heavy. Closing my eyes, drowning out my thoughts, concentrating on my goal for tonight, I don't hear Liam talking to me.

"The guys should be down in the lobby already, are you going to be good douche?"

Opening my eyes, I catch the last part of what he was saying.

"Forgive me already, I don't know what I was doing. I just... I just didn't think. I'm sorry." Not wanting him pissed off at me, or this interfering between us.

"I owe you one. Remember that. I will forgive you. But when the time comes, and I need to fucking punch you in the face, you better forgive."

He smiles, like he already has the when and where planned. I disregard his comment knowing that no matter what, I would forgive him.

Doors opening to the elevator, the guys, Gage, Zepp, and Jason are there waiting. I put my hand back on Liam's shoulder using him as my feet.

"Ready to fucking party?" I growl. Needing to get this want for the Minx out of me in a seriously bad way. All eyes on me. They start laughing. They had identified that I am besotted with tequila.

My lovely, lovely lifelong friend.

I remind them of the bet and also that I am still up by one. Winning. They groan, then give back fighting remarks how they, except for Liam, are all going to have five-some orgies tonight. I start laughing with roar but not because I doubt them. If anyone could do it, easily it would be us.

We don't chase pussy. Pussy chases us. But imagining every single one of them having orgies in their hotel rooms tonight. If only the Self-righteous Natalie could see us now. Then she would really know what she has gotten herself into. What fold she has been sucked into. It would be priceless.

We would corrupt her soul, rip it out, stomp on it, and shred it again and again. We are all Free-Lancers in the commitment department. Simply forming a bond with each other. There is no room for a flighty unstable brunette. It would be best for her to learn it sooner than later.

Stepping outside the hotel, a black stretch limousine, is already waiting for us. Probably Gages doing. The guy is always prepared, I was set on taking a cab. Liam shoves me in head first. I fall onto the seats body askew; the guys start laughing and climb in sitting on opposite seats.

"So where to?" I ask questioning.

If they have planned to have a limousine outside waiting for us then surely they've planned where we are going.

"We're headed to New Scotland Ave, there's a club there. A Popular party scene that holds a lot of willing pussy." Gage says eyes glinting.

"Great, just what I need."

Liam looks to me, his lips in a deterred sneer. Of all people, he is the last person I would expect to see judging. My Minx has something on him, on me, a chain, and a hold. She needs to let the fuck go.

Pulling up to some cheesy fucking club, the guys all get out ahead of me. As I crawl out Liam grabs my hand and yanks me with him. "Dude there's no hand-holding inside, got it? We are here to get women, not scare them off." I say, leaning into him. Riling him up.

"Well if you could've controlled yourself, and waited to sample the alcohol until we arrived, I wouldn't have to hold your hand." He replies snarling. Pulling my hand back, away from him as if he burned me.

"You're not my fucking babysitter, go find yourself a God damn woman and leave me alone." I reply.

He goes too far sometimes, touching boundaries he should stay away from. Storming away, I weave back and forth passing everyone who has been waiting in line. Budging ahead, I approach the club bouncer. Taking a couple hundred dollar bills out of my pocket I slyly hand it to him, and he lifts his all-important red-rope letting me in. The guys can bribe their way in themselves. People start mumbling obscenities because I jumped ahead. Being rich and famous does have some good qualities. Such as never having to wait in a forever long line. Not glancing a look at any female I pass by, I walk right up to the bar. Before I even get my hand halfway in the air to signal that I need service the hot little bartender approaches me.

Pushing her breasts together, almost falling out of her barely there tank-top. I force myself to keep my eyes focused on hers. It's a game I enjoy playing at immensely. I play hard to get. They put themselves out there on a platter over and over, until I notice. Only, I know I came here with one intention, to get a female who is doing just that, what she is doing right now.

Teasing me with what I can have, what I will have. I order a shot of Whiskey, one after another. Hot little bartender makes a pit stop in front of me.

"I am free after two, if you're lonely."

Thinking of Natalie, angered by where my mind goes constantly.

"I'll think about it." She saunters off, shaking her ass with every step.

Quarter after two. Camp still set up at the bar. The guys have long disappeared with women. Liam too, surprisingly. Maybe I could have made a rash decision thinking something was there between him and the Minx.

Not that it's my business what they do.

In the past couple of hours, while downing shots, I have learned that hot bartenders name is Leslie. She also wants to make it far away from New York, and she wants to fuck me. Simple, common groupie qualities. Although the way her lithe body moves, I'm betting I'll be getting the better part of this deal. Unwilling to give her anything but one night, one night that she is about to lose if she doesn't get her ass out here soon. I'm ready to head back to the hotel.

Throwing some cash down on the bar. I push the stool back and lead my footsteps in the direction of the exit. Only steps to fresh air and a lit cigarette hands wrap around my hips. I turn my head back looking over my shoulder at Leslie. I grin at her.

"Going somewhere without me?" She asks, a little too insecurely for my liking. Second guessing what the fuck I am doing, I hesitate in replying. Fuck it.

"Just out for a cigarette until you were ready, your shift end yet?"

"Already clocked out, I am all yours." She purrs, trying to be sexy.

It wasn't.

Stepping outside, forgoing the smoke I had planned. She hails a cab. I tell her I am staying at the Hilton. She tells the cab driver. Arriving at the hotel entrance I give the cab driver the fee, including a large tip. My privacy expected. I get out before her and walk around the car to open her door, she steps out one leg at a time.

"Follow me" I whisper. Doubting if I could do this when really all I want to taste and feel is my Minx. I walk to the elevator, not stopping or looking behind me to see if she is following. When I step inside the elevator and press the third floor button, she wraps her arms around me again. I'm doing everything within my power not to shrug her off.   My body tenses trying to rein control.

No one touches me without myself initiating contact. This one-nighter is already trying my boundaries'. The elevator doors slide apart. She lets go, and I step off.   Her trailing behind. I stop in front of my door. Before opening, I glance down the hallway, making sure Liam nor are Natalie's doors open, chancing them seeing me.

Presuming the coast is clear, I slide my keycard in and the door clicks. I push the door open and step to the side allowing Leslie entrance before me.

"Drink?" I offer her.

"Sure, I'll have whatever you're having." She says, sliding her arms back around my waist. This time her hand creeping to the front of my jeans, unbuttoning.

CHAPTER EIGHTEEN

Steele

𝒥umping away from her, while dropping the miniature shot bottle I had in my hand.

"Are you all right babe?" she asks curiously.

I need to get the fuck out of here, right now. Something is seriously wrong with me; I am declining a willing pussy. Instead, inside, I am shaken and stirred over the Minx.

"Yeah, I'm fine, uh why you don't make yourself a little more comfortable while I run down to the lobby."

Noticing that I had spilt the last of the liquor I had while jumping away from her blunt ministrations.

"I'm going to get us some drinks." I say on a fake promise.

Closing my room door, assured that I have nothing of value or personal in that room, a lesson from the past learned. I lean my body up against my door hoping the one-nighter doesn't come looking for me. I look to my left knowing its Natalie's room. For the second time this day, fuck it.

Approaching her door, second guessing if I should knock. Should I do this? Walk into this possible fucking mess. Would I be satisfied would she be satisfied with only one night? Can I consciously break her this completely? This thing between her and me, it has to end. We cannot go another seven weeks like this. On the borderline of hate and encompass. Making my choice, I lift my hand up enclosed it in a fist and knock.

CHAPTER NINETEEN

Natalie

*L*aying on my side, blanketed in sheets and comforters, saddened to feel so alone, and left behind. I hear a loud knocking on the door, who the hell could this be at three o'clock in the morning? Getting out of bed and shrugging on my robe, I open the door.   Ryan Fucking Hurst. Clearly intoxicated with the smell radiating off of him is beyond powerful, I was wondering if one could become inebriated by scent of alcohol alone.

"Yes?" I ask irritatingly.

"Can I come in? We need to talk." Ryan says. Trickily asking but an underlying demand laced in his tone.

"I have no reason to talk to you. Unless it's about my internship or the tour. We have nothing to say to each other." I say shaking my head showing that this isn't up for discussion. Suddenly I am pushed back. Ryan shoving his way into my room. Locking my door behind him, this man clearly has an issue with the word no. Either he doesn't know the meaning or just doesn't listen.

"What in the hell do you think you are doing? Ryan, I think we played this game earlier, and it ended just as it should have." I say, slowly putting space between us and wrapping my arms around myself with chills zapping at my skin.

"You see, Minx, this is where I think you are wrong." He says, coming at me.

Glint in his eye, and a sloppy stumble in his step. I keep backing up until my legs hit the bed. I know there is nowhere else to run. I'm stuck in this position. Ryan holding the expression of a hunter on his face and I am his prey.

CHAPTER TWENTY

Steele

I've got her just where I want her. Nowhere to run, nowhere to hide. We will be done with this right here and now. I lean in as close as I can without touching her. But oh, how I want to. Want to run my tongue along the seam of her luscious pouty lips wrap my fingers tightly in her hair and pull her to me.

But this, this is going to be slow and torturous. If I kiss her now, I know I won't be able to hold off from being inside her immediately. I'm going to strum this out for as long as I can. The longest guitar solo ever played. The lyrics, her moans.

Overcome by greed, I fulfill my cravings taking her all in. Inches away from my touch, she's trembling. Her hair mussed from bed. A white cotton robe concealing her curves, reaching her knees that I am holding back from ripping off her. Lust in her eyes undoubtedly, for me. Saving time, I pull my shirt off over my head. She continues to stare while remaining mute. Taking turns, her eyes slowly get their fill of me.

My hair free sculpted chest. My eight pack of abdominal muscles that I faithfully work hard to keep. I unbuckle my belt and unbutton and unzip my pants, letting them slowly drop to the floor pooling around my feet, stepping out of my jeans I kick them to the side. Grabbing her hands, I push them to her side. Untying her robe, I let the sash fall. Her robe slightly agape. I can see she has nothing on underneath; I want more than anything to rip it away from her body. But I can't, she has to come to the decision on her own. I want her full consent.

Nervous as fuck that she's going to tell me to get out. I stand there holding my hands at my sides clutched in fists, wearing nothing but my boxer briefs. If she cannot tell how much I want her at this moment, if she cannot see how hard it is for me to stay pliant. Then there is no hope for tonight. For this to happen.

She slowly brings her hands up, gripping at the opening of her robe. I suck in my breath, holding it until I notice she's deliberately delaying.

This Minx is teasing me.

I laugh out loud, causing her to insecurely close the gap. Reassuring her, I place my hands upon hers.

"I need you." I say with an unrecognized gruff. My emotions wavering through the air.

Our fingers become interlaced and together we slide her robe off. Leaving her eyes, I look down. My Minx is an angel. Supple and soft in all the imaginable right places. She is nothing I expected. Her breasts are more than a handful and her nipples area pale pink puckered begging for my wet rapacious kiss. Hips, enough for me to grab onto for leverage, and her pussy bare.

I look back into her eyes, subliminally conveying how much I want, how much I fucking need her. And then we combust. Her hands ripping at my hair wrapping around me. At the same time I pull her to me, wrapping her hair around one hand and grabbing her ass pushing her into me, so she can feel how fucking hard my cock is for her.

I lift her up and gently set her on the bed, throwing the comforter and sheets to the side at the same time. Climbing over her, I kiss her neck. Nipping, licking my way to her beautifully pink tinted areolas. Taking turns nipping and sucking at each nipple, her breathing coming in short rasps.

Continuing to pinch and rub her hardened nipples. I kiss her hip, her stomach and every untouched spot on her body. Making love to her skin, so unlike me. My cock, hidden in my briefs is ready to explode. Slowly, I spread her legs placing small kisses from her ankle to her inner thigh. Her pussy is soaking, dripping wet. Perfectly pink, slowly tracing circles around her clit. Teasing her, she moans out my name. Making me only want to be as deep inside of her as possible. Inserting one finger, she's so fucking tight. She begs for more; she's undoing me.

Leaning forward while pushing my finger in and out of her, I taste her. Her legs shaking; she pushes my head closer to her pussy her moans pleading for me to continue. Who am I to deny her needs? My tongue lapping at her, adding another finger. I suck her clit frantically, and I gently fuck her with my fingers and she suddenly comes apart, screaming my name and her body trembling. Pulling my hair.

I hop off the bed, grabbing my jeans searching for a condom in my pocket I had placed there hours before. I yank my briefs off, and tear the foil off the packet and glide the condom on over my cock. Placing my knee between her legs, kneeling over her somehow finding my voice. I ask; no I beg for her consent.

There's no going back from this.

"Do you want me?" I ask, nervous as to what her answer will be.

"Please....Yes...Yes...Fuck Ryan ...Yes," she shoves out on a breath.

Positive she has no doubts; I put my other knee between her legs. Spreading hers as far apart as they can go, placing the head of my cock on her lips. I slide it up and down over her slit. Rubbing her juices all around, basking in the wetness of her.

She wraps her hands in my hair, pulling me to her, placing rough open mouth kissed on my lips.

"Just fucking do it Ryan" she whispers against my mouth.

And Fuck if I didn't slam it in at the end of her words. Her body tense beneath me, I didn't know she was a fucking virgin. How did I not fucking see this? I yell at myself. Even if I did though, I still would have wanted her, if not much more.

I stay still frozen inside of her as long as I can so she can adjust to my swelling cock inside of her. I'll be damned that some part of me was overjoyed there has been no one before me in her.   She rubs her hands over my ass, my back, clutching at my shoulders.

"Ryan, move will you."

Satisfied that her body has slowly relaxed, I pick of a steady pace, thrusting in and out of her soaking wet pussy.

She's clawing at my back, rasping breaths, whispering in my ear how good my cock feels. My release hanging by a thread on a cliff. Needing her to come before I do, I reach my hand down between our bodies and start rubbing her clit. Roughly kissing her at the same time. She starts moaning against my lips.

Begging for more, I feel her pussy walls clenching my cock. Her pussy vibrating in orgasm is my unraveling. My seed, shooting out of my cock by an unknown force. Catching my breath while still inside of her, I look her in the eyes. Un-Fucking-believable. That was the sex we just had. Fucking mind-blowing.

Unsure if it meant the same to her as it did me. I leave my cock inside of her, making it a somewhat awkward position, not wanting this moment to end, not wanting to forget how her pussy feels. Her eyes, blinking, opening slower and slower. She's going to pass out; I've fucked her to sleep. That's a first. Carefully sliding out of her, not wanting to cause her to wince in pain.

I stand up and walk to the bathroom. Ripping the used condom off I throw it in the toilet and flush. Finding a washcloth, I put it under warm water, squeeze it out, so it's not sopping wet, I walk back into the room. Sensitively cleaning her, she will be sore in the morning. I throw the washcloth on the bathroom floor, slide her over on the bed and lie down next to her. Holding her close. Breathing her scent in.

I stare at her peaceful sleeping form, wondering what has happened to her to make her so cold, so broken, but in bed the warmest, most reactive person I have ever had sex with.

CHAPTER TWENTY ONE

Natalie

*W*aking up with a start, I look around. I am alone. Of course, it would have been a one-time thing. Why or even how could I have ever thought any different? Set on giving him a piece of my mind, I look around for my cell phone. Finding it, I send a text to Liam, asking him what floor and room Steele is in. Liam replies in seconds seems Ryan's room is right next door. I am not going to let him just walk away from this, what we did. I know it affected him as deeply as it did me.

I could see the truth in his eyes. He was nervous last night. He owned me with his body.

I take a fast shower and then get dressed, making myself presentable enough to argue, I'm sure if I didn't have clothes on we wouldn't be able to settle this. I leave my room and start knocking on his door. No answer. Are you fucking kidding me? He thinks I will leave if he doesn't answer. Think again. I resume my pounding, after minutes the door opens.

My mouth drops, blinking repeatedly, when that doesn't work I pinch myself. This can't be fucking real. My gut churns, nausea running a weave throughout. My heart erratically thumping in my chest and pain, lacing a needle around it. I stutter.

"Is Steele here?" the beautiful brunette answers me.

"Honey, my turn isn't over why don't you come back tomorrow?"

Trying to ignore the fact that she is completely naked, her hair is a fucking mess and her make-up is running. She looks like she was just thoroughly fucked.

By Steele.

I can't even reply. I storm back to my room, not wanting her to see my uncontrollable tears. Grabbing my cellphone, I pull up a travel search website and book a flight home. To Boston. Grabbing my overnight bag and sitting the hotel room keycard on the nightstand. I run. They can send my other clothes after me; I'm not risking a chance at seeing anyone on the bus. I exit the hotel undiscovered, and luckily there is a cab waiting at the exit. I tell the cab driver to take me to Albany International Airport while throwing him some cash.

CHAPTER TWENTY TWO

Steele

*U*nable to sleep hours later, my thoughts running wild about this amazingly unpredictable woman cocooned in my arms. Something passed between us tonight. It was more than sex. Much more. I need to digest this. Away from her. Her being around inhibits me from thinking straight.

Slowly unwrapping my arms, trying not to disturb her beautiful sleeping form, I disengage my arm from under her. Covering her with the blankets I search for my clothes. Putting them back on and taking one last glance at her I leave her room.

Not wanting to deal with the situation in my room, hoping she took it upon herself to find her way out. I head downstairs, outside to have a smoke. Your thoughts are better sifted through with a clear, unbiased mind. An employee part of hotel personnel security stops me when they see I am smoking. Pointing me in the direction of where the smoking spot is. Apparently customers prefer non-smoking hotels and the smoking area to be hundreds of feet away from the entrance.

I step up into the round gazebo that has one commercial ashtray situated in the middle. Fortunately it's so damn early in the morning no one else is here. No one to recognize who I am. Sitting down on one of the benches I inhale my fix. There is no way I can allow my Minx to be a one-time thing. Last night, I can't even think of any possible words that could form a coherent sentence to describe what happened between us.

I could write a song about that one moment, where everything changed. I don't want to settle down; that's not for me. I also don't want to let her go; I don't want to let her ignore what we have. The thought of her running back to Liam, even if it's just for some semblance of comfort, it makes me sick. God- I am a selfish prick.

Throwing my cigarette in the ashtray, I decide I can't wait for this conversation between her and me to happen. I have to wake her up. Waiting will just allow my thoughts to fester and grow. When we checked in, I made sure to get a master key for all of our rooms. Something I did ever since Gages orgy in my room.

Unlocking her door, I see that the bed is empty. Check the bathroom. Empty too. I sit on the bed. Maybe she went to get something to eat or back to the bus for a change of clothes. After waiting for a half an hour, I run down to the parking lot, knowing that's where she has to be.

Searching the entire tour bus, her shit is still here but she isn't, I'll check her room again. She has to be back by now, Stepping into her room it's the same as it was when I left a few moments earlier. Angered, I just start throwing shit. The TV, the lamps, anything nearby that I can get my hands on. Running my hands through my hair, think, where the fuck could she have gone? I run out of her room and start pounding on Liam's door. He opens immediately.

"Where the fuck is she?" I yell while grabbing his throat and pinning him against the wall.

"Who?" He yells back.

"Natalie! Where is she? Are you hiding her?" I scream, squeezing his throat harder.

"Calm the fuck down. I haven't seen her since yesterday. Why are you acting like this?" His breath coming out short.

I know he is telling the truth. I would know if he were lying. He's the worst liar.

I slowly unlock the hold I have around his neck. Checking my pocket for my phone, I remember I left it in my room. Suddenly I find myself running across the hall, unlocking and opening my door. I don't even realize Hot Bartender is still here, shoving my clothes around in my overnight bag I find what I am looking for.

As I drop my bag, phone in hand and ready to call Natalie. I stole her number from her School transcripts. Leslie speaks, shocking me out of my revelry of finding my phone.

"I didn't think you were coming back, but I'm pretty happy that you did. I was hoping that Brunette creature didn't run into you."

I drop the phone from my hand.

"What!"

CHAPTER TWENTY THREE

Natalie

*R*unning out of the airport, wanting to be home already. The pain that has consumed me since the leftover-lover opened his door is just too much. For the past five years of my life, my soul has been consumed by copious amounts of pain. I'm tired, exhausted of waking up every morning, only to remember.

No one understands what it is like, walking throughout life a shadow of my former self, my soul having been stolen. My heart in a constant ache, music being my only haven. That haven was stolen last night. Music notes, lyrics, rhythm, a beat, that's what passed between us. We wrote a song. Together. Pulling up to my and Layla's apartment, I see that her car isn't in the parking lot.

Thanking whoever is out there up above. I couldn't handle seeing her right now. She would be pissed that I came back. But I am not a fighter. I run away from anything that could get rough. And I just can't deal anymore. I can't.

Unlocking our apartment door, I frantically run into Layla's room, into her bathroom. Knowing that she has a prescription bottle of the opiate Oxycodone, desperate for this pain to be gone.

I find what I am looking for. Pushing down on the safety lock, I turn the cap, dump a handful in my hand and place the bottle back in her medicine cabinet. One hand full of pills I turn the faucet on, closing my eyes I say a prayer. God just please, please take it away. This pain it's just too much. Take it all away. Forgive me. I cup my hand under the water, tossing the pills down my throat and swallowing them with a gulp of water.

I run into my room and grab a notebook. I have to write Layla a note so she can somehow find a way to move on. So she can live her life guilt free. She has always been a fighter. My fighter, as well. She shouldn't have to be one for me though. Knowing I won't have long before the medicine works its way into my bloodstream, I begin writing with a shaky hand.

Dear Layla,

You will never know how much I love you and for that I am sorry. I am sorry I've done this, but I didn't have a choice. I'm just sick Lal. I just can't do this anymore. I'm so tired of hurting; I've made it so long with this ache and it's become too unbearable. I don't want you to hurt. This isn't your fault or anything you could have prevented. I just need to do this. I will see you again; I promise. I love you. Forever.

Nat

Sitting the notebook on my nightstand, my eye lids start getting heavy, my breathing shallow and my body slowly starts becoming lethargic. Pulling the picture of my parents out of my pocket, I lay down on my bed and hug the photo to my chest. So very comfortable. I keep my eyes closed and drift off to sleep…

"Are you at all haunted by memories past? Are you ready to make this one breathe your last? Is your chest so heavy you're ready to leave? Or are you just hoping that someone will grieve?"

-The Amity Affliction

DEDICATION

This book is for all of the loves in my life. Yes, I've several.

Chad, my soul mate. You truly complete me. Thank you for keeping Boog busy so I could write. Your playlist inspired me, so stop with the "I told you so." Also, your headphones are way better. Forever and Evers.

Payton, the little one who inherited the all of my best qualities. I do this for you. I love you.

Tina, My Bina, My Wifey. The one who gave me that first push, more like a shove into doing this. You've been reading along as I wrote, even when I made massive errors, and you still fell in love with it. Here's to deciding what to be.

Amber, My sister. I think you've gotten pissed at me more than once throughout this story. I'm sorry. You'll forgive me soon; you have to. To him.

Mary, we talked about this for years, and you have always been a supporting friend and reader. I did it!!!

Kirstie and Maeghan, even though you're not fans of the reading world, and more than once threatened to delete me off of Facebook because of my constant posts. You've still supported me. Also, I want to kiss those lips.

Carl, with that one text you made me cry, here's to hoping it happens.

My parents, if it wasn't for you both forcing me to read every single night, I don't think I would have ever fallen in love with books. Thank you.

To Music, I would be insane without you, you inspire me every day to write another word. You break my soul open and free it. I will forever love you.

More from A L Wood

An excerpt from Last Chance: Rock Romance #2

Prologue

Layla

*J*ust getting off from my eight hour shift at the hippest local bar in Boston, I'm exhausted and ready to hit my bed full force. Luckily, I had a day shift so it wasn't nearly as busy as it is when working the night shift. I can't get Nat out of my mind. In the past week, I have only heard from her once.

When I dropped her off she promised me she would stay in contact. This is the longest we will be away from each other since we've been alive. I also know this is way out of her comfort zone. The members of *"Steele's Army"* are daunting and I know she puts on a tough exterior act but she can only hold that facade up for so long.

I couldn't help but push her into this. After five years of seeing her live her life hidden beneath this shell, as her best friend, I refused to stop being her enabler. She ought to have so much more than what life has thrown at her, forced upon her. I know my parents; my father more so, feels extreme guilt.

I also know that since the tragedy Nat has never blamed my dad. I have never needed her confirmation; we have always been a family. The accident ruined my dad. He killed his best friend, his brother and his wife.

After that day, he could never keep eye contact with me; a big part of the reason I agreed and supported Nat's decision to leave New York. I was tired of my family not being able to linger around me for more than ten minutes. They thought that money could somehow substitute their absence.

Do I enjoy the money? Is it cold in Antarctica?

I enjoy not having to rely on student grants or loans to pay for college. I also enjoy not having to wonder where my next paycheck is going to come from and worry over how each bill will get paid. I like being able to help people, others that are not as fortunate as I.

I enter the apartment throwing my car keys down on the kitchen counter, too lazy to attempt at cooking something to eat, I throw ramen in the microwave. While my food is cooking I decide to go into Natalie's room. This week has been agony for me. Being without her here in this apartment isn't the same. It's lonely without her music jamming loudly at all hours of the day, hell it's just lonely without her.

I've probably slept in her room four nights this week. Finding comfort by enfolding myself in her blankets. Our lives were planned to be intertwined long before we were born. Natalie will always be my other half. A part of my being. She has always felt that I was her sanity, her reason to keep moving every day. She's always voiced her opinion on that.

What she doesn't know is that I feel an overbearing guilt at what my father did. Accident or no. If my dad had just suggested they call a taxi, her parents would still be here. She wouldn't be as closed off as she is now. She wouldn't be severely heartbroken trudging along in life. Sometimes I think she can see through me. See why I do what I do. She puts on the hard shell to her exterior never letting anyone in but me. I do the opposite. I have let people in all the time. But only for a few nights of fun. Those few nights allow me to feel alive again. But I am not deserving of feeling alive.

So when the guilt makes its way in, slowly creeping along my soul. That's when I kick them out of my bed. To be honest, they don't deserve it either. If I let someone in, and let them know how much I ache for Natalie, how much hate and disgust I have for my parents or how much these thoughts consume me, they would only look at me with indifference. No one could or would ever understand.

I open her bedroom door and straight away notice she's laying in her bed.

What the fuck?

Why is she here in her room?

She should be on a tour bus right now. How the hell did she get here?

I walk over to her bed and start shaking her awake. She doesn't respond. I shake her again, this time a little harder.

"Nat!" I yell out.

"Natalie!"

Her not responding to me has my stomaching overturning. To set my mind at rest, I lay my head on her chest, just to hear her heartbeat. It's beating, slowly. I start screaming her name out loud. Hoping, no praying that she will answer me or make some kind of movement. Her face is abnormally pale.

I jump off the bed and yank my cellphone out of my pocket, furiously dialing 911. *Natalie what did you do?* The dispatcher answers the call. Rushing the words out I tell her my friend is laying in her bed not responding to anything I do and that her heart is barely beating. She tells me she's sending an ambulance. That everything will be all right.

Right now I am having a very hard time accepting that everything will be okay. I have never seen Natalie like this.

What happened?

As the dispatcher is still on the phone, she directs me to check Nat's pulse. To keep checking it to make sure she hasn't stopped breathing altogether. Sitting on the bed beside Natalie's body with my thumb on her wrist, I glance at her nightstand and notice a piece of paper sitting there.

A letter. Addressed to me. Oh Natalie. She did this on purpose.

Now available on Amazon!

An excerpt from *Honestly Unfaithful*

Chapter One

Maggie

"This is bullshit," I say out loud to no one in particular, not that anyone is listening anyway. I'm new here, haven't even had a chance to check out the local hot spots, so to everyone around me I am invisible.

When you decide to move halfway across the country and transfer into a college where everyone knows each other, you're bound to be stared at while sitting in the waiting room of the administration office at Duke University.

It's not like I wanted to move nearly three thousand miles away; Jake had left me no choice. Jake was my boyfriend, as in past tense.

Was.

I thought I had it all mapped out. I'd end up marrying my now ex-long-term boyfriend one day. We'd have two children, and we'd live in a modest house while maintaining successful careers. All before we were thirty.

Jasper, Indiana wasn't a large city, and unless you've heard of Scott Rolen—chances are, you haven't heard of Jasper, either. There, everyone knows everyone. Jake and I grew up together, started dating in middle school, and graduated head over heels in love. We agreed to take a year off after high school.

We traveled all over the United States for that year, Jake's parents covering every expense as a part of our graduation gift. When our year was up, we found a small one-bedroom apartment, moved in together, and began college.

That's where our future began going slowly downhill.

It was little things at first. Twenty-one questions if I came home late from a night of studying with a group; accusations if I had to stay later at work. Then, before I knew it, his issues escalated. He lost all the trust he had for me and wanted to control everything I did, all of the time. It was like a switch was flipped the day I signed my name with his on the lease for our apartment.

I made excuses.

That it was just his way of showing me how much he cared.

Excuses upon excuses.

Until the night I ran.

Months of one-sided arguments blew the fuck up. I was always so busy studying or working or being the great girlfriend, that I wanted a break. Just one night out with my girlfriends—Jake knew about it. I had to tell him the exact bar I would be in, the time I would arrive there, and the time I would be leaving. He had to know how I would get home and at what precise time I would be walking through the front door. Everyone's numbers were to be left with him in case he couldn't reach me via my cellphone.

It was ludicrous, all of it.

But I did it anyway, because I loved him and I was determined to make us work.

Flash forward: I'm at the bar and it's fifteen minutes past the time I said I would be getting home. I unlocked my cell phone to send Jake a text, letting him know that I was sorry for being late and I was on my way. I'm greeted with eighty-seven missed phone calls and fifty-eight unread text messages.

All from Jake.

Instead of calling or sending him a text message, I decided to just leave the bar, grab a cab, and get my ass home.

I predicted that being late would mean I was going home to an all-night one-sided argument where I would have to defend that I was a twenty-one-year-old college student with a boyfriend. Not an old shut-in lady.

I wasn't expecting his visceral anger.

When I got home, Jake must've been stewing. Before I knew it, Jake had grabbed hold of me and slammed my head into the wall numerous times. Before I blacked out, the first thought I had was, *This is not the man I fell in love with.* When I finally stirred awake, I found my wrists tied to the frame of our bed. He was lingering over me with his hands raised as if he were to hit me. *I flinched*; I didn't want him to hit me again. But he gestured and screamed in my face that he "wasn't going to ever let me step foot out of the apartment again, for as long as he lived."

I knew I had to find a way to leave. His promise to keep me locked away forever was a real fear.

I was tied to that bed for two long, arduous days, left to sit in my own filth as punishment for my "transgression" of disobeying his order to come home right away.

I manage to convince him I wouldn't leave the house ever again.

Luckily, he had classes and I was untied. I packed the necessities as fast as I could and ran. Ran as far away as I could before he could find me.

Now, here I am, waiting to see someone in administration about graduating this year with my degree.

"Margaret Whitaker?" a middle-aged woman with glasses calls out my name.

I follow behind her, taking a seat in the chair across from her desk.

"I see that you are a new transfer and are wanting to graduate a semester early. Is that correct?" she asks while glancing at my transcripts.

"Yes, that's correct."

"Well, to be honest, looking at your files, you're on the right path for earning all of your credits to graduate early. The only thing that will be in your way is that you need to have a completed internship."

"An internship?"

"Yes, although it is kind of late to apply for one, coincidentally I have had an opening to an internship in the physiology department under Professor Jackson."

"But my major doesn't have anything to do with physiology," I argue. "Please, I need to graduate."

They should let me graduate by default because they can't offer an internship that goes along with my degree.

I can see the sympathy etched on her face. Maybe my desperate pleas will help? "It doesn't have to, honey, you can intern anywhere. As long as you do the internship and receive a letter of completion it will go toward your credits for graduation. Professor Jackson is one of the nicer professors to intern under. He will be patient with you since he knows you are majoring under another department. Now, you can apply and see what will come of it, or you can go back to your dorm room and try to figure this out for yourself. What's it going to be?"

I shuffle my feet, trying to decide. Having made up my mind, I look back up and reach out for the application.

Available on Amazon!

ABOUT THE AUTHOR

A.L. Wood resides in Glens Falls, NY with her husband and daughter. When she's not writing she's reading and spending time with her family and friends.

A.L. Wood can be found on Facebook and twitter, both links are below if you are interested in keeping up with any new releases.

https://www.facebook.com/ALWood

https://twitter.com/ALWoodAuthor

Made in United States
Troutdale, OR
02/02/2024